雅典文化

MP3

基礎篇

脫口說英語

Daily English Conversation

張瑜凌 著

EASY ENGLISH
EASY TALK

國家圖書館出版品預行編目資料

脫口說英語 / 張瑜凌編著

-- 二版. -- 新北市：雅典文化，民108.02

面； 公分. -- (全民學英文；51)

ISBN 978-986-96973-4-7 (平裝附光碟片)

1. 英語　　2. 會話

805.188　　　　　　　　107021865

全民學英文系列 51

脫口說英語

編著／張瑜凌

責任編輯／張瑜凌

美術編輯／王國卿

封面設計／林鈺恆

法律顧問：方圓法律事務所／涂成樞律師

總經銷：永續圖書有限公司　　　CVS代理／美璟文化有限公司
永續圖書線上購物網　　　　　TEL：（02）2723-9968
www.foreverbooks.com.tw　　FAX：（02）2723-9668

出版日／2019年02月

雅典文化

出版社	22103　新北市汐止區大同路三段194號9樓之1
	TEL　（02）8647-3663
	FAX　（02）8647-3660

脫口說英語，是再簡單也不過的事！

臨時遇到要說英文的場合，你該如何應對呢？千萬不要只想著趕緊逃離現場或挖個地洞鑽進去！如果不是要長篇大論的用英語發表言論，那麼「脫口說英語－基礎篇」便是您最得力的語言好幫手了。

不論是公司外籍客戶來訪、認識外籍朋友、在路上遇到需要幫助的外籍人士等，您都可以輕輕鬆鬆哈拉一兩句，既不會面臨啞口無言的尷尬場面，更免於失禮的窘境。

「脫口說英語－基礎篇」規劃八大情境會話，再搭配本書所附的學習光碟，跟著外籍老師逐句練習，就可以應付需

要簡單對話的場合。

此外,本書更編撰「延伸用法」及「相關用法」兩大單元,沒有冗長的使用解釋,只要您跟著學習光碟開口大聲念,一樣可以達到學習相關情境的用法!

Chapter 2 辦公室

Chapter 3 電話

Chapter 4 購物

Chapter 5 人際關係

Chapter 6 客套短語

Chapter 7 交通

Chapter 8 問路

Chapter 1 生活常用

Unit 01 碰到熟人

Hi, Jenny.

嗨,珍妮。

David : Hi, Jenny.

嗨,珍妮。

Jenny : Hi, David. Where are you going?

嗨,大衛。你要去哪裡?

David : I'm going to pick up my wife.

我要去接我太太。

Jenny : How is Helen?

海倫好嗎?

David : She's great. Thank you. And you?

她很好。謝謝。妳呢?

Jenny : Not bad. I've got to catch my bus.

不錯。我要去趕我的公車了。

David : OK. See you.

好的。再見囉!

0
1
7

1 生活常用

2 辦公室

3 電話

4 購物

5 人際關係

6 客套短語

7 交通

8 問路

延伸用法

- Hello.

  哈囉！

- Hi, there.

  嗨，你好。

- Hey.

  嘿！

- Hello, guys.

  哈囉，各位。

相關用法

- Good morning.

  早安！

- Good afternoon.

  午安！

- Good evening.

  晚安！

Unit 02 剛認識打招呼

Nice to meet you.

很高興認識你。

David : Great party, isn't it?
很棒的宴會，是吧？

Helen : Yeah, it is.
是啊，的確是。

David : My name is David White.
我的名字是大衛‧懷特。

Helen : Nice to meet you, Mr. White.
很高興認識你，懷特先生。

David : Just call me David. And you are?
叫我大衛就好。那妳是？

Helen : Sorry, I'm Helen.
抱歉，我是海倫。

David : Where are you from, Helen?
妳從哪裡來的，海倫？

Helen : I'm from Taiwan.
我來自台灣。

延伸用法

- Nice to meet you too.
  （我也）很高興認識你。
- Nice to meet you again.
  很高興再次見到你。
- Nice to see you.
  很高興認識你。
- Nice to see you too.
  （我也）很高興認識你。
- Nice to see you again.
  很高興再次見到你。
- Glad to see you.
  很高興認識你。

相關用法

- It's nice to meet you.
  很高興認識你。
- I'm glad to meet you.
  我很高興認識你。
- My pleasure to meet you.
  能認識你是我的榮幸。

Unit 03 從事的工作

What do you do?

你從事什麼工作？

Helen : Nice to meet you, David.
很高興認識你，大衛。

David : Nice to meet you too.
（我）也很高興認識妳。

Helen : What do you do?
你從事什麼工作？

David : I am a teacher.
我是老師。

Helen : Really?
真的？

David : And what about you?
那妳呢？

Helen : I am an editor.
我是一位編輯。

David : Oh, are you?
喔，妳是啊？

① 生活常用

2 辦公室

3 電話

4 購物

5 人際關係

6 客套短語

7 交通

8 問路

延伸用法

- What do you do exactly?
  你到底從事什麼工作？

- What do you do for a living?
  你以什麼維生？

- What do you do, if I may ask?
  如果不介意我問，你從事什麼工作？

- What's your job?
  你的工作是什麼？

- What's your occupation?
  你的職業是什麼？

- What business are you in?
  你從事哪一行？

相關用法

- What's your position?
  你的職位是什麼？

- Whom do you work for?
  你為誰工作？

- Where do you work?
  你在哪兒工作？

Unit 04 問候

How do you do?

你好嗎?

Jack : Good morning, Sean.
早安,西恩。

Sean : Good morning, Mr. White.
早安,懷特先生。

Jack : Please call me Jack.
請叫我傑克。

Sean : How do you do, Jack?
你好嗎,傑克?

Jack : I am fine, and yourself?
我很好,那你呢?

Sean : Not so good.
不太好。

Jack : What happened?
發生什麼事了?

Sean : I broke up with my girlfriend.
我和我女朋友分手了。

延伸用法

- How are you?
  你好嗎?
- How are you doing?
  你好嗎?
- How are you going today?
  今天過得如何?
- How have you been?
  你最近怎樣?
- How is everything?
  你好嗎?
- How is it going?
  事情都還好吧?

相關用法

- How are things going?
  事情進展得怎樣?
- How is your wife?
  嫂夫人好嗎?
- How is your family?
  你的家人好嗎?

Unit 05 回應問候

I'm doing fine.

還可以。

Sean : Jack?
傑克？

Jack : Hi, Sean.
嗨，西恩。

Sean : How are you doing, pal?
你好嗎，伙伴？

Jack : I'm doing fine, thank you.
還可以，謝謝你。

Sean : How about Jenny?
珍妮好嗎？

Jack : She is good, too.
她也很好。

Sean : Good to see you.
真高興見到你。

Jack : Yeah, me too.
是啊，我也是。

0 2 5
1 生活常用
2 辦公室
3 電話
4 購物
5 人際關係
6 客套短語
7 交通
8 問路

延伸用法

- I'm doing great.

  我過得不錯。

- I'm fine.

  我很好。

- I'm OK.

  我還過得去。

- I'm pretty good.

  我蠻好的。

- I'm exhausted.

  我累壞了！

- I'm busy now.

  我現在很忙。

相關用法

- Nothing special.

  沒什麼特別的。

- Not too bad.

  不太壞。

- So far so good.

  目前為止都還好。

Unit 06 邀請

How about Chinese food?

要不要吃中華料理？

David: Are you busy now, Jenny?
珍妮，妳現在忙嗎？

Jenny: No, not at all.
沒有，完全不會。

David: Are you doing anything tonight?
妳今天晚上有事嗎？

Jenny: No, nothing special. Why?
沒有，沒什麼特別的事。怎麼啦？

David: Do you feel like having dinner with me?
妳想要和我一起吃晚餐嗎？

Jenny: Sure, why not?
當然好，為什麼不要呢？

David: How about Chinese food?
要不要吃中華料理？

Jenny: That's a good idea.
好主意。

延伸用法

- How about this one?
  這個如何？

- How about a drink?
  要喝一杯嗎？

- How about Sunday?
  星期天如何？

- How about yourself?
  你自己呢？

- How about seeing a movie?
  要不要去看電影？

- How about going for a walk?
  要不要去散散步？

相關用法

- Sounds great.
  聽起來不錯。

- That's terrific.
  不錯啊！

- That would be fine.
  好啊！

Unit 07 發生什麼事？

What's up?

發生什麼事了？

David : My God!
　　　　我的天啊！

Jenny : You look upset.
　　　　你看起來很沮喪喔！

David : So obviously?
　　　　有這麼明顯嗎？

Jenny : What's up?
　　　　怎麼啦？

David : I think I failed my math test.
　　　　我想我的數學考試考砸了。

Jenny : I'm so sorry to hear that.
　　　　很抱歉聽到這件事。

David : I shouldn't go to see a movie last week.
　　　　我上星期不應該去看電影。

Jenny : You did? No wonder.
　　　　你有去喔？難怪！

延伸用法

- What happened?

  發生什麼事了？

- What happened to you?

  你發生什麼事了？

- What's the matter?

  發生什麼事了？

- What's the matter with you?

  你發生什麼事了？

- What's wrong?

  怎麼啦？

- What's happening?

  發生什麼事？

相關用法

- Are you OK?

  你還好吧？

- Something wrong?

  有事嗎？

- Is everything OK?

  凡事還好吧？

Unit 08 請問貴姓

What's your name?

你叫什麼名字？

David: What a great movie, isn't it?
很棒的電影，是吧？

Jenny: Yeah, it is.
是啊，的確是。

David: I'm David. What's your name?
我是大衛。妳叫什麼名字？

Jenny: Hi, David. I'm Jenny.
嗨，大衛。我是珍妮。

David: Hi, Jenny. Nice to meet you.
嗨，珍妮。很高興認識妳。

Jenny: Me, too.
我也是。

David: Where are you from?
妳來自哪裡？

Jenny: I'm from Canada.
我來自加拿大。

延伸用法

- What's your name again?
  你說你叫什麼名字？
- What should I call you?
  我要怎麼稱呼你？
- May I have your name?
  請問你的大名？
- You are?
  您是？
- Your name, please?
  請問大名？
- How should I pronounce your name?
  你的名字要怎麼發音？

相關用法

- What's your last name?
  你貴姓？
- Are you Mr. White?
  你是懷特先生嗎？
- How do you spell your name?
  你的名字要怎麼拼？

Unit 09 感謝

Thank you.

謝謝你。

Helen : Excuse me.

抱歉！

David : Yes?

什麼事？

Helen : Where is the post office?

郵局在哪裡？

David : You go straight down this street to the corner.

妳往前直走，一直到街角。

Helen : Go straight down. And then?

往前直走。然後呢？

David : It's on the right side of the street.

就在街道的右邊。

Helen : Thank you.

謝謝你。

David : You are welcome.

不客氣。

0 3 3

1 生活常用
2 辦公室
3 電話
4 購物
5 人際關係
6 客套短語
7 交通
8 問路

延伸用法

- Thanks.

  謝啦!

- Thanks a lot.

  多謝!

- Thanks again.

  再次謝謝!

- Thank you anyway.

  總之,還是要謝謝你!

- Thank you so much.

  非常感謝!

- Thank you for everything.

  謝謝你為我所做的一切。

相關用法

- It's very nice of you.

  你真好!

- I don't know how to thank you.

  我不知道要如何感謝你。

- I really appreciate it!

  我真的很感激!

Unit 10 介紹自己

I am David White.

我是大衛・懷特。

David: Hi, I'm here to meet Mr. Smith.
嗨，我來見史密斯先生。

Helen: May I have your name, please?
請問您的大名？

David: I am David White.
我是大衛・懷特。

Helen: Please have a seat, Mr. White.
請坐，懷特先生。

David: Okay.
好的。

Helen: I'll tell Mr. Smith you are here.
我會告訴史密斯先生您來了。

David: Thank you so much.
感謝您。

Helen: You're welcome.
不客氣。

0
3
5
1 生活常用
2 辦公室
3 電話
4 購物
5 人際關係
6 客套短語
7 交通
8 問路

延伸用法

● I'm David.
我是大衛。

● My name is David.
我的名字是大衛。

● Please call me David.
請稱呼我大衛。

● Just call me David.
叫我大衛就好。

● David White.
（我是）大衛・懷特。

● David White, by the way.
順帶一提，（我是）大衛・懷特。

相關用法

● This is my wife Jenny.
這是我的太太珍妮。

● Joe, this is my wife Jenny.
喬，這是我太太珍妮。

● Come to see my wife Jenny.
來見見我的太太珍妮。

Unit 11 願意

No problem.

沒問題！

Jenny: Are you busy now, David?
　　　　大衛，你在忙嗎？

David: Not at all. Why?
　　　　一點都不會。怎麼啦？

Jenny: Would you do me a favor?
　　　　你可以幫我一個忙嗎？

David: No problem. What's it?
　　　　沒問題！是什麼事？

Jenny: How do you pronounce it in
　　　　English?
　　　　這個英文怎麼發音？

David: Let me see...it's strategy.
　　　　我看看…是 strategy。

Jenny: I've got it. Thank you.
　　　　我懂了。謝謝你。

David: You are welcome.
　　　　不客氣。

延伸用法

- Yes.

  是的！

- OK.

  好！

- Sure.

  可以啊！

- Of course.

  當然！

- No sweat.

  沒問題！

- As you wish.

  就照你的意思！

相關用法

- I'd love to.

  我願意！

- Keep going.

  繼續(說或做)。

- Go ahead.

  去做吧！

MP3 012

0
3
9

1 生活常用

2 辦公室

3 電話

4 購物

5 人際關係

6 客套短語

7 交通

8 問路

Unit 12 不願意

I don't think so.

我不這麼認為。

Jenny: Where is the stapler?
釘書機在哪裡？

David: It's on the table.
在桌子上。

Jenny: Really? But I can't find it anywhere.
真的嗎？可是我到處找不到。

David: I said it's on the table.
我說在桌子上。

Jenny: On the table? Can you find it for me?
在桌子上？你可以幫我找嗎？

David: No, I don't think so.
不，我不這麼認為。

Jenny: Oh, come on.
喔，拜託！

David: OK. You owe me one.
好吧！你欠我一個人情。

延伸用法

- No, I don't want to.
  不，我不想要。
- No, I don't think so.
  不，我不這麼認為。
- No, I won't.
  不，我不要。
- I'm afraid not.
  恐怕不行。
- That's impossible.
  不可能。
- No way.
  想都別想。

相關用法

- Of course not.
  當然不好。
- Don't think about it.
  想都別想。
- No, thanks.
  不用，謝謝！

Unit 13 道歉

I'm terribly sorry.

我非常抱歉。

David：Look at the pictures.
看看那些畫。

Jenny：How amazing.
真是令人感到驚奇。

Cathy：Hey, watch out.
喂，小心點！

David：What's wrong?
發生什麼事？

Cathy：You stepped on my toes.
你踩到我的腳了。

David：I'm terribly sorry. Are you OK?
非常抱歉。妳還好吧？

Cathy：No problem.
沒關係。

0
4
1

1 生活常用

2 辦公室

3 電話

4 購物

5 人際關係

6 客套短話

7 交通

8 問路

延伸用法

- Sorry.
  抱歉。
- I'm sorry.
  抱歉。
- I'm really sorry.
  真的很抱歉。
- My mistake.
  我的錯。
- It's my fault.
  是我的過失。
- Please forgive me.
  請原諒我。

相關用法

- Never mind.
  不用在意。
- It's OK.
  沒關係。
- It's no big deal.
  沒什麼大不了。

Unit 14 時間

What time?

幾點？

Jenny: Hi, David How are you doing?
嗨，大衛。你好嗎？

David: Great. Look, do you have any plans tonight?
不錯。聽著，今晚妳有事嗎？

Jenny: Tonight? Nope. Why?
今天晚上？沒事！怎麼啦？

David: Mark and I are going to see a movie. Would you like to come?
馬克和我要去看電影。妳要來嗎？

Jenny: I'd love to. What time?
我願意！幾點？

David: Let's see.... We'll pick you up at five.
我想想…。我們五點來接妳。

Jenny: Great. See you then.
好。到時候見。

0 4 3

1 生活常用
2 辦公室
3 電話
4 購物
5 人際關係
6 客套短語
7 交通
8 問路

延伸用法

- What time is it now?

  現在幾點了？

- Time is up.

  時間快到了。

- It's about time.

  時間到了！

- It's time to call him.

  是該打電話給他的時間了！

- Does anyone know what time it is?

  有誰知道幾點了嗎？

- Is five o'clock OK?

  五點可以嗎？

相關用法

- Oh, it's too late.

  喔，太晚了。

- Time is running out!

  沒有時間了！

- Hurry up. We're late.

  快一點。我們遲到了。

MP3 015

Unit 15 請求提供幫助

Would you do me a favor?

你能幫我一個忙嗎？

Jenny : Busy now?

現在忙嗎？

David : A little bit.

有一點。

Jenny : Would you do me a favor?

你能幫我一個忙嗎？

David : What's it?

什麼事？

Jenny : Please move this box for me.

請幫我移這個箱子。

David : Sure.

當然好。

Jenny : And pass me the file, please.

還有，請把檔案夾遞給我。

David : Here you are.

給你。

延伸用法

- Please help me.
  請幫助我。
- Give me a hand, please.
  請幫助我。
- I need your help.
  我需要你的幫助。
- I need some help.
  我需要一些幫助。
- Please do me a favor.
  請幫我一個忙。
- Can you help me?
  你能幫我嗎？

相關用法

- Are you busy now?
  你現在忙嗎？
- Are you in the middle of something?
  你在忙嗎？

Unit 16 好久不見

It's been a long time.

好久不見。

David: Jenny, is that you?
珍妮，是妳嗎？

Jenny: Hi, David. It's been a long time.
大衛！好久不見。

David: How have you been?
妳好嗎？

Jenny: Just fine. And you?
還不錯！你呢？

David: Great. Gee, it's great to see you. And how is John?
很好。嘿，真是高興見到妳。約翰好嗎？

Jenny: Oh, he's OK. How about your family?
喔，他不錯。你的家人好嗎？

David: Everyone is doing great.
每個人都不錯。

0 4 7
1 生活常用
2 辦公室
3 電話
4 購物
5 人際關係
6 客套短語
7 交通
8 問路

延伸用法

- Hi, long time no see.
  嗨,好久不見了。
- I haven't seen you for ages.
  好久不見了!
- I haven't seen you for a long time.
  好久不見了!
- It's been so long.
  好久不見。
- When did we meet last time, you remember?
  我們上次見面是什麼時候?你記得嗎?

相關用法

- Where have you been?
  你都去哪啦?
- You look great.
  你看起來氣色真好。
- You haven't change at all.
  你一點都沒變。

Unit 17 祝福

Say hi to John for me.

幫我向約翰問好。

David: How is John?
約翰好嗎?

Jenny: He's fine, thanks.
他很好,謝謝。

David: I've got to go. Can I give you a call?
我要走了。我可以打電話給妳嗎?

Jenny: Yeah, sure.
好啊,當然可以!

David: Say hi to John for me. OK?
幫我向約翰問好,好嗎?

Jenny: I will.
我會的。

David: See you later.
再見囉!

Jenny: Bye.
再見!

1 生活常用
2 辦公室
3 電話
4 購物
5 人際關係
6 客套短語
7 交通
8 問路

延伸用法

- Say hi to him for me.
  幫我向他問好。
- Tell him I miss him.
  告訴他我想念他。
- Give my love to John.
  幫我向約翰問好。
- Give my best to John.
  幫我向約翰問好。
- Have a nice weekend.
  週末愉快。
- Have a nice time.
  祝你快樂。

相關用法

- Please give my regards to John.
  請幫我向約翰問好。
- Take care.
  保重。
- Take care of yourself.
  你自己要保重。

Unit 18 道別

Good-bye.

> 再見!

David : Why don't you come over for dinner sometime?
妳何不找時間來吃晚餐?

Jenny : I will.
我會的。

David : You promise?
妳保證?

Jenny : Sure. OK, nice talking to you.
當然。好了,很高興和你聊天。

David : Me too.
我也是。

Jenny : Take care.
保重啦!

David : You too! Good-bye!
你也是!再見!

Jenny : Bye.
再見!

1 生活常用
2 辦公室
3 電話
4 購物
5 人際關係
6 客套短語
7 交通
8 問路

延伸用法

- See you.

  再見!

- See you soon.

  再見!

- See you around.

  再見!

- I'll see you later.

  再見!

- So long.

  再見!

- So long for now.

  先説再見囉!

相關用法

- Take care.

  保重!

- Catch you later.

  再見!

- Don't be a stranger.

  別變陌生人。(要保持聯絡)

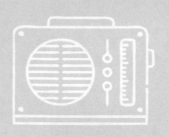

Chapter
2 辦公室

Unit 01 有訪客

May I help you?

需要我幫助嗎？

Helen: May I help you?
需要我幫助嗎？

David: Has Mr. Jones come back?
瓊斯先生回來了嗎？

Helen: Did you have an appointment?
您有先約嗎？

David: We're supposed to have a meeting at two o'clock.
我們兩點鐘有個會議。

Helen: Mr. Jones said he would be back soon.
瓊斯先生說他馬上會回來。

David: He's late again.
他又遲到了。

Helen: Do you mind waiting a few minutes?
您介意稍等片刻嗎？

David : No problem.
　　　沒問題。

延伸用法

- Can I help you?
  需要我幫忙你嗎？
- How can I help you?
  我要如何幫你？
- How may I help you?
  我要如何協助你？
- What can I do for you?
  我能為你做什麼嗎？
- Yes?
  有事嗎？

相關用法

- Sir?
  先生？（有事嗎？）
- Madam?
  女士？（有事嗎？）

Unit 02 介紹新人

It's **David**'s first day today.

今天是大衛第一天上班。

1 生活常用

2 辦公室

3 電話

4 購物

5 人際關係

6 客套短語

7 交通

8 問路

Helen : Brian, this is David. David, this is Brian.

布萊恩，這是傑克。傑克，這是布萊恩。

David : How do you do?

你好嗎？

Brian : Great. Good to have you, David.

很好。很高興有你加入，大衛。

Helen : It's David's first day today.

今天是大衛第一天上班。

Brian : You look familiar.

你看起來有一些面熟。

David : Yeah, you too.

是啊，你也是。

延伸用法

- This is our newest team staff David.

  這是我們新進的成員大衛。

- I want you to meet the newest member of our team.

  我要你來見見這位我們小組的新進成員。

- I want to introduce our newcomer David.

  我想要介紹我們新成員大衛。

- David just started working today.

  大衛今天開始上班。

相關用法

- He'll be part of our marketing department.

  他即將是我們行銷部門的一份子。

- He just started yesterday in marketing.

  他昨天才剛開始行銷的工作。

Unit 03 新人自我介紹

I'm the new assistant.

我是新的助理。

David: Hi, I'm the new assistant. Just call me David.

嗨，我是新的助理。叫我大衛就好。

Helen: Welcome, David.

歡迎，大衛。

David: I'm glad to be on board.

我很高興能加入這個團隊。

Helen: We are lucky having you.

真幸運有你加入我們。

David: It's my honor.

是我的榮幸。

Helen: If you need any help, just let me know.

假使你需要任何幫助，告訴我一聲。

David: Thank you.

謝謝妳。

延伸用法

- I'm David.

  我是大衛。

- It's nice to meet you.

  很高興認識你。

- My name is David Jones.

  我的名字是大衛‧瓊斯。

- Please call me DJ.

  請叫我DJ。

1 生活常用

Unit 04 新人到職

I'll show you around.

我帶你四處看一看。

2 辦公室

Helen: It's nice to have you with us.
很高興你加入我們。

David: Me too.
我也很高興。

3 電話

Helen: I'll show you around.
我帶你四處看一看。

David: I appreciate your help.
謝謝你的幫忙。

4 購物

Helen: Listen, you'll find working here very pleasant.
聽著，你會發現在這裡工作是非常快樂的。

5 人際關係

David: I think so too.
我也是這麼認為。

6 客套短語

Helen: Do you have any questions so far?
目前為止你還有任何問題嗎？

7 交通

David: Not for now.
現在沒有。

8 問路

延伸用法

- Working here is a big challenge.
  在這裡工作是一個很大的挑戰。

- You'll soon find that you have a very good supervisor.
  你很快就會發現,你有一位非常好的主管。

- This Sales Marketing Department is a high-pressure world.
  這個行銷部門的壓力很大。

- I want to formally welcome you to the company.
  我要正式歡迎你加入公司的行列。

- I hope you will be happy here.
  希望你在此一切滿意。

相關用法

- Do you have any questions?
  你有任何問題嗎?

- Let me know if you need help.
  如果你需要幫助,讓我知道一下。

Unit 05 工作代班

Could you cover for me on Friday?

你星期五能不能幫我代班？

David: Can you talk for a minute?
有空聊一聊嗎？

Helen: Sure. What's up?
好啊！什麼事？

David: Could you cover for me on Friday?
妳星期五能不能幫我代班？

Helen: But I switched with Chris.
但是我跟克里斯換班了。

David: Oh, no.
喔，糟糕。

Helen: What happened?
怎麼啦？

David: I'm going to meet my wife at the airport.
我要去機場接我太太。

Helen: Why don't you ask Jason for help?
你怎麼不試試找杰生幫忙？

1 生活常用
2 辦公室
3 電話
4 購物
5 人際關係
6 客套短語
7 交通
8 問路

延伸用法

- Could you cover for me on this weekend?

  你這個週末能不能幫我代班？

- Mark will take over my regular duties.

  馬克會代理我的工作。

- Jack is covering for me Saturday.

  傑克星期六會幫我代班。

- Who will do my regular duties?

  誰要做我例行的工作？

相關用法

- Can you help me?

  你能幫我一個忙嗎？

- Can you help me with it?

  你能幫我這個嗎？

MP3 024

0
6
5

1 生活常用

2 辦公室

3 電話

4 購物

5 人際關係

6 客套規題

7 交通

8 問路

Unit 06 工作討論

Can I talk to you?

我可以和你說話嗎?

David: Can I talk to you?
我可以和妳說話嗎?

Helen: Sure. Have a seat.
當然可以。坐下吧!

David: I'd like to discuss with you about the advertisement.
我想要和妳討論有關廣告的事。

Helen: It's a lot of hard work.
這工作很不簡單。

David: The board is meeting to discuss the company's problems.
董事會要開會討論公司的問題。

Helen: We have to think up a way to solve this problem.
我們必須想一個辦法來解決這個問題。

延伸用法

- Do you have a minute?

  你有空嗎？

- Can I talk to you now?

  我現在能和你說話嗎？

- Can I talk to you for a moment?

  我能和你談一下嗎？

- Can you talk for a minute?

  有空聊一聊嗎？

- Are you free to talk now?

  你現在方便說話嗎？

- Is this a good time to talk?

  現在方便說話嗎？

相關用法

- Are you busy now?

  你現在在忙嗎？

- I need to talk to you.

  我需要和你聊一聊。

Unit 07 工作細節

What's your point?

你的重點是什麼？

David: When is the project due?
計畫案截止日是什麼時候？

Helen: This Friday.
這個週五前。

David: Well, I'm afraid I couldn't finish it in time.
是喔，我擔心我無法及時完成。

Helen: What's your point?
你的重點是什麼？

David: I've got so much to do.
我有很多事情要做。

Helen: Why wouldn't you start this project today?
為什麼你不今天就開始這個計畫？

David: Yes, sure. That's what I usually do.
是啊，當然。我通常就是這麼做的。

延伸用法

- Would you get to the point?
  能不能把重點說得更清楚一點？
- What are you trying to say?
  你要表達的是什麼？
- What do you mean?
  你的意思是什麼？
- What document are you talking about?
  你指的是什麼資料？

相關用法

- Tell me the details.
  告訴我細節。
- Am I missing something?
  我有錯過什麼（重點）嗎？

Unit 08 工作交辦

When do you want me to finish it?

你希望我什麼時候完成？

Helen : Are you in the middle of something, David

大衛，你在忙嗎？

David : No, I'm not.

沒有，我沒有。

Helen : Would you type the report for me?

能幫我把報告打好字嗎？

David : Sure. When do you want me to finish it?

好的。妳希望我什麼時候完成？

Helen : By two o'clock.

兩點鐘前。

David : But I've got to finish a report by two.

但是我兩點鐘前要完成一份報告。

Helen : It's OK. Just finish this report today.

沒關係。只要今天之內把這份報告完成。

David : I'll.
我會的。

延伸用法

- I'll do that right now.
  我馬上去做。
- Let's get started.
  我們開始吧!
- Let's get down to work.
  開始工作吧!
- I promise to finish this report by two.
  我答應兩點鐘前完成這個報告。
- I'll do my best to deal with it as quickly as possible.
  我會盡我的能力盡快處理。
- I'll get my job done on time.
  我會準時把工作做完。

相關用法

- When can I get started?
  我什麼時候可以開始呢?
- When should I finish it?
  我應該什麼時候完成呢?

Unit 09 工作執掌

I'm going to run an errand for Mr. Jones.

我要幫瓊斯先生跑腿做一件事。

Helen : Hey, how is everything?

嘿，還好吧？

David : So far so good.

目前為止還不錯。

Helen : Are you busy now?

你現在忙嗎？

David : Kind of busy. I'm going to run an errand for Mr. Jones.

有一點忙。我要幫瓊斯先生跑腿做一件事。

Helen : But you're not his secretary.

但是你不是他的秘書。

David : Yeah, I know. But I'm his younger brother.

是啊，我知道。但是我是他的弟弟啊！

延伸用法

- I'm in charge of it.
  我負責這件事。
- I'll make travel arrangements for my boss.
  我要幫我的老闆安排旅遊事宜。
- I'll be a great assistance to this project.
  我會是這個計畫的得力助手。
- I have to finish my paperwork before 3 o'clock.
  我必須在三點鐘前完成我的文書工作。

相關用法

- I've finally cleared up some problems.
  我終於解決了一些問題。

Unit 10 行程安排

Let me check his schedule.

我來確認一下他的行程。

David: Mr. Jones won't have a break until two o'clock, I guess.

我猜一直到兩點鐘,瓊斯先生都不會有空。

Helen: But I have an appointment with Mr. Jones at five.

但是我和瓊斯先生約五點鐘。

David: I know. Mr. Jones has got a pretty tight schedule today.

我知道。瓊斯先生今天行程很滿。

Helen: When will Mr. Jones come back?

瓊斯先生什麼時候會回來?

David: Let me check his schedule.

我來確認一下他的行程。

Helen: Thanks.

謝啦!

延伸用法

- Mr. Jones's plane is timed to arrive at four o'clock.

  瓊斯先生的飛機預計四點鐘抵達。

- Mr. Jones will have a meeting with David over lunch.

  瓊斯先生和大衛有一個午餐會議。

- From three until five, I have to attend a senior staff meeting.

  從三點鐘到五點鐘，我要參加高層管理人員的會議。

- Could you arrange this meeting on Friday morning?

  你能安排這個會議在星期五早上嗎？

相關用法

- Can we meet on Tuesday?

  我們星期二可以見面嗎？

- Please set up a meeting with Mr. Jones for me.

  請幫我安排和瓊斯先生見面。

Unit 11 工作量太大

Can't you see my hands are full?

你沒看見我的手上一堆事嗎?

Helen: In the middle of something?
正在忙嗎?

David: Can't you see my hands are full?
妳沒看見我的手上一堆事嗎?

Helen: Hey, come on. You have to take a break.
嘿,好了。你應該要休息一下的。

David: There's too much work.
真的太多工作了。

Helen: You have been working overtime since last week.
從上個星期開始,你一直都在加班。

David: I'm a little frustrated about my job.
我對我的工作有點挫折感。

Helen: Listen, do you want some coffee?
聽著,你要來杯咖啡嗎?

David: That would be great.
太好了。

延伸用法

- I'm overwhelmed with a heavy workload.
  我的工作量真的超出負荷了。
- I've got so much to do.
  我有一堆事情要做。
- There is a lot of work piled up on my desk.
  我桌上的工作堆積如山。
- I've been overworking.
  我一直工作太過度了。
- I'll have to work overtime tonight.
  我今晚要加班。

相關用法

- Don't you think you should take a vacation?
  你不覺得你應該休假嗎？
- You should take a vacation.
  你應該要休假。
- I got two weeks' leave.
  我獲得兩週的假期。

Unit 12 正忙於工作

I'm busy connecting my clients.

我正忙於聯絡我的客戶。

David : Can I talk to you for a moment?
我能和妳說一下話嗎？

Helen : No, you can't.
不，你不可以。

David : It won't keep you long.
不會耽擱妳太久的時間。

Helen : But I'm busy connecting my clients.
但是我正忙於聯絡我的客戶。

David : Just a minute, please?
只要一分鐘就好，拜託？

Helen : OK. What's it?
好吧！什麼事？

David : I suppose I'll have to look for a new job.
我應該要再找一份新工作。

Helen : What for?
為什麼？

延伸用法

- I'm in the middle of something.
  我正在忙。
- I'm tied up at the moment.
  我在忙走不開。
- I'm busy at work.
  我忙著工作。
- I'm really busy at the moment.
  我現在真的非常忙。
- I'm extremely busy.
  我非常的忙。
- I'm in a bit of flap.
  我有點慌亂。

相關用法

- I can't leave this job at the moment.
  我目前必須做這個工作無法走開。
- Sorry. No more time to talk.
  抱歉。沒時間說話。

Unit 13 行政庶務

Where did you keep the files?

你把檔案都放在哪裡了？

David : Excuse me, Helen.
海倫，請問一下。

Helen : Yes?
有事嗎？

David : Where did you keep the files?
妳把檔案都放在哪裡了？

Helen : You ask the wrong person. I didn't keep it.
你問錯人了。不是我收的。

David : Then who did it? What a mass here.
那是誰收的？這裡真亂。

Helen : My boss did. He is a micromanager.
我的老闆收的，他是事必躬親。

David : I see. I'm going to ask him instead.
我瞭解，我改去問他好了。

Helen : He's in his office.
他在他的辦公室。

延伸用法

● I send Mr. Jones a follow up email.
我寄給瓊斯先生一封追蹤進度的電子郵件。

● Please do it all over again.
請重新再做一次。

● Please start over from the beginning.
請重新再做一次。

● Fax this paper to Mr. Jones.
把這份文件傳真給瓊斯先生。

相關用法

● Can you write it down?
你能記下來嗎？

● Can you type this letter for me?
你能幫我打這封信嗎？

Unit 14 請假

He took a day off.

他請了一天假。

Brian : How come David didn't come in today?

大衛今天怎麼沒來上班？

Helen : He took a day off.

他請了一天假。

Brian : How is David's work?

大衛的工作表現如何？

Helen : Excellent.

很棒。

Brian : Really? Look, can you keep a secret?

真的？聽好，妳能保守秘密嗎？

Helen : I won't say anything.

我不會說出任何事的。

Brian : It's between us. David is going to quit tomorrow.

就我們兩人知道就好。大衛明天就要辭職了。

延伸用法

- I'm off today.
  我今天休假。
- I'm taking a couple of days off next week.
  我下禮拜要請幾天假。
- I need a sick leave for 2 days.
  我需要請兩天病假。
- I took a day off because of illness.
  我因病請了一天假。

相關用法

- How many personal days do I have?
  我還有幾天事假可以請？
- I'll take 4 days off.
  我要請四天假。

Unit 15 人事規定

Did you punch in?

你上班打卡了嗎？

Helen : You are late again.

你又遲到了。

David : I'm so sorry.

我很抱歉。

Helen : The rules pretty relaxed here....

這裡的規定並不嚴…。

David : I know what you mean. I won't do it again.

我知道你的意思。我不會再犯。

Helen : Good. Did you punch in?

很好。你上班打卡了嗎？

David : Not yet.

還沒有。

Helen : Just do what you have to do now.

趕緊去做你應該做的事。

延伸用法

- I forgot to punch out.

  我忘記下班打卡了。

- Today is payday.

  今天發薪水。

- There are some formal rules in our company.

  在我們公司有些正式的規定。

- I'd like to request my travel reimbursement.

  我的旅費需要報帳。

- They were paid extra for overtime.

  他們拿到了加班費。

- We don't need to punch in and out here.

  我們這裡(公司)不必打卡。

Unit 16 辦公室軟硬體

My computer kept crashing.

我的電腦一直當機。

David : Oh, no.

喔,不會吧!

Helen : What's wrong?

發生什麼事?

David : My computer kept crashing.

我的電腦一直當機。

Helen : You've got a virus on your system.

你的系統中毒了。

David : Not again?

不會再來一次吧?

Helen : What happen now?

現在又怎麼啦?

David : My computer won't boot up.

我的電腦無法開機。

延伸用法

- My computer is too slow.
  我的電腦速度太慢。
- The monitor is wavy.
  螢幕老是在閃。
- How do I change fonts?
  我要怎麼更換字型？
- How do I get it to print?
  我要怎麼列印？
- This copier is broken.
  這台影印機壞了。
- May I use your telephone?
  我能借用你的電話嗎？

相關用法

- It's out of paper.
  沒紙了。
- My pen is out of ink.
  我的筆沒水了。
- I can't find my white-out.
  我找不到我的修正液。

Unit 17 同事代為留言

She will call back later.

她等一下會回電。

Helen : Hi, David. I'm back from lunch.
嗨，大衛。我午餐吃完回來了。

David : How was your lunch?
午餐吃得如何？

Helen : Hmm, so-so. Did anyone call?
嗯，馬馬虎虎啦！有人打電話來嗎？

David : Yes. Someone name Cathy Jones.
有的。一個叫做凱西‧瓊斯的人。

Helen : What did she say?
她有說什麼嗎？

David : She will call back later.
她等一下會回電。

Helen : OK.
好。

延伸用法

- She wants you to call her back.
  她要你回電。

- She can't meet you tonight.
  她今晚無法和你見面。

- She wants you to call her back at work.
  她要你工作時間回電給她。

- She didn't leave a message.
  她沒有留言。

- She's in town until Sunday.
  一直到星期天她都會在城裡。

相關用法

- She's staying at her brother's, and you can reach her after 6pm.
  她會在她兄弟家裡，你可以晚上六點之後聯絡到她。

- She has some questions about your order.
  對於你的訂單她有一些問題。

Unit 18 午餐休息

I really need a break.

我真的需要休息一下。

Helen: Did you have lunch?
你有吃午餐嗎？

David: No, I didn't have time.
沒有，我沒有時間。

Helen: Why don't you go out now?
你為何不現在出去？

David: But I'm too busy now.
可是我現在太忙。

Helen: I'll take over for you.
我來幫你代理。

David: Really? I really need a break.
真的嗎？我真的需要休息一下。

Helen: No problem. Go ahead.
沒問題啦！去吧！

David: Thanks a lot.
多謝啦！

延伸用法

● I'm so tired.

我好累喔！

● I'm exhausted.

我累壞了。

● I'm going out later.

我等一下要出去。

● I'll go out for lunch.

我要出去吃午餐。

● I need to eat something.

我需要吃一點東西。

● I'm just going to get a sandwich.

我要去吃三明治。

相關用法

● Would you like to have lunch with me?

你要和我一起吃午餐嗎？

Chapter
3 電話

Unit 01 去電找人

Is Chris around?

克里斯在嗎？

David: IBM corporation. May I help you?
這是 IBM 公司。我能幫你什麼嗎？

Helen: Is Chris around?
克里斯在嗎？

David: Let me take a look.
我看一下。

Helen: Sure.
好的。

（稍後）

David: He's at his desk. Wait a moment. I'll put you through.
他在座位上。請稍等。我會幫妳轉接。

Helen: Thank you.
謝謝你！

延伸用法

- Is Chris there?
  克里斯在嗎？
- Is Chris in today?
  克里斯今天在嗎？
- Is Chris in the office now?
  克里斯現在在辦公室裡嗎？
- I need to talk to Chris.
  我要和克里斯通電話。
- This is James calling for Chris.
  我是詹姆士打電話來要找克里斯。

相關用法

- Hello, may I speak to Chris?
  哈囉，我能和克里斯說話嗎？
- May I speak to Chris, please?
  我能和克里斯說話嗎？
- Could I talk to Chris or Sunny?
  我能和克里斯或桑尼說話嗎？

Unit 02 本人接電話

Speaking.

請說。

David : Hello?

哈囉?

Helen : Hi. May I speak to Mr. David White?

嗨。我能和大衛‧懷特先生講電話嗎?

David : Speaking.

請說。(我就是大衛‧懷特)

Helen : Oh, hi, Mr. White. This is Helen. I'm calling to discuss our annual plans with you.

喔,嗨,懷特先生。我是海倫。我打電話來和您討論我們的年度計畫。

David : OK. What can I help you?

好的。有什麼我能幫忙妳的嗎?

延伸用法

- This is Kate Simon.

  我是凱特‧賽門。

- This is she.

  我就是你要找的人。（適用女性）

- This is he.

  我就是你要找的人。（適用男性）

- It's me.

  我就是。

- I can't talk to you now.

  我現在不能講電話。

- I am really busy now. I'll call you later.

  我現在真的很忙。我待會打電話給你。

相關用法

- Who is calling, please?

  你是哪一位？

- Would you mind calling back later?

  你介意等一下再打電話過來嗎？

Unit 03 請來電者稍候

Hold on, please.

請稍等。

Helen : Hello?

哈囉？

David : Hi, Helen? This is David.

嗨，海倫？我是大衛。

Helen : Oh, hi, David. How are you doing?

喔，嗨，大衛。你好嗎？

David : Not bad. Is Mr. Martin around?

不錯。馬丁先生在嗎？

Helen : Yes, he is.

是的，他在。

David : Please tell him I called.

請告訴他我來電。

Helen : OK. Hang on, please.

好的。請等一下。

David : Thanks.

謝謝！

1 生活常用

2 辦公室

3 電話

4 購物

5 人際關係

6 客套招呼

7 交通

8 問路

延伸用法

- Hold the line, please.

  請稍等不要掛斷電話。
- Wait a moment.

  等一下。
- Just a minute, please.

  請等一下。
- Would you wait a moment, please?

  能請你稍等一下嗎？
- Would you mind holding for one minute?

  你介意稍等一下嗎？
- Could you hold the line, please?

  能請你稍等不要掛斷電話嗎？

相關用法

- Could you hold for another minute?

  你能再等一下嗎？
- The line is busy, would you like to hang on?

  電話忙線中，請別掛斷好嗎？
- Can you hold?

  你能等嗎？

Unit 04 感謝對方稍候

Thank you for waiting.

謝謝你等這麼久。

Helen: Thank you for waiting. Susan is still on the phone. Could you hold for another minute?

謝謝你等這麼久。蘇珊還在電話中。你要再等一下嗎？

David: Sure, I'll wait.

好的，我會稍等。

Helen: Thank you.

謝謝你。

（稍後）

Susan: Hello, David? Sorry, I'm still on the phone. I'll call you back in 20 minutes, OK?

哈囉，大衛？抱歉，我還在電話中。我廿分鐘後回你電話好嗎？

David: OK. Remember to call me back.

好吧！記得要回我電話。

1 生活常用
2 辦公室
3 電話
4 購物
5 人際關係
6 害羞短語
7 交通
8 問路

延伸用法

- I have got a call.

  我要接一下電話。

- Why don't you stay on the line?

  你能在線上等著嗎？

- Sorry to have kept you waiting.

  抱歉讓你久等了。

- I'm sorry to have kept you waiting.

  我很抱歉讓你久等了。

相關用法

- I'm sorry for the delay.

  抱歉這麼晚才來接電話。

- There is the phone. I'll get it.

  電話響了。我來接。

- I'll be right back.

  我會馬上回來。

Unit 05 代接電話

Let me see if he is in.

我看看他在不在。

David: This's David calling. Is Jenny around?

我是大衛。珍妮在嗎？

Helen: Let me see if she is in.

我看看她在不在。

David: Thank you.

謝謝你。

Helen: You are welcome.

不客氣。

（稍後）

Helen: I'm sorry, David, but she's still on the phone.

抱歉，大衛，但是她還在講電話。

David: Would you tell her to answer my call?

可以請妳轉告她先接我的電話嗎？

Helen: OK. Wait a moment, please.

好的。請等一下。

延伸用法

- I am sorry, but he is busy with another line.

  很抱歉，他正在忙線中。

- Wait a moment, please. I'll get him.

  請稍等，我去叫他。

- You can try again in a few minutes.

  你可以過幾分鐘再打來看看。

- Who is calling, please?

  請問你是哪一位？

- I'll connect you.

  我幫你轉接電話。

- Would you like to hold?

  你要等一下嗎？

相關用法

- Which Tom do you want to talk to?

  你要和哪一個湯姆說話？

- Do you know his extension?

  你知道他的分機嗎？

Unit 06 受話方在何處

Where is he?

他人在哪裡?

David: I'd like to speak to Nelson.
我要和尼爾森講電話。

Helen: I'm sorry, but he is not at his desk.
很抱歉,但是他不在他的座位上。

David: Where is he? Is he off today?
他人在哪裡?他今天休假嗎?

Helen: I'm not sure. Would you like to leave a message?
我不確定。你要留言嗎?

David: Sure. This is David and tell him to return my call, OK?
好的。我是大衛,然後告訴他回我電話好嗎?

Helen: OK. I'll give him the message.
好的。我會告訴他留言。

延伸用法

- Do you have any idea where he is now?

  你知道他現在在哪裡嗎？

- Do you know when he would come back?

  你知道他什麼時候會回來嗎？

- Do you know when he will be back?

  你知道他什麼時候會回來嗎？

- Do you know where I can reach him?

  你知道我在哪裡可以聯絡上他嗎？

相關用法

- When will he come back?

  他什麼時候會回來？

- Is he off the line?

  他講完電話了嗎？

- May I have his phone number?

  可以給我他的電話號碼嗎？

Unit 07 受話方在忙線中

He's on another line.

他正忙線中。

David : May I speak to Johnny?
　　　　　我能和強尼講電話嗎？

Helen : He's on another line. May I take a message?
　　　　　他正忙線中。要我幫你留言嗎？

David : OK. Would you tell him I called?
　　　　　妳能告訴他我來電過嗎？

Helen : Of course. Who should I say is calling?
　　　　　當然好。我要説是誰來電？

David : I'm David Jones.
　　　　　我是大衛・瓊斯。

Helen : OK, Mr. Jones, I'll tell him you called.
　　　　　好的，瓊斯先生，我會告訴他你來電。

David : Great. Thank you.
　　　　　很好。謝謝妳。

延伸用法

- He's busy with another line.

  他正在另一條線上（講電話）。

- His line is busy now.

  他現正忙線中。

- Your party is on the line.

  你要找的人現正忙線中。

Unit 08 受話方不在

He is in a meeting now.

他現在正在開會中。

David：Good morning. May I help you?
早安。有需要我服務之處嗎？

Helen：Hello, may I speak to Chris? This is Helen.
哈囉，我能和克里斯說話嗎？我是海倫。

David：I'm sorry, but he is in a meeting now.
抱歉，他現在正在開會中。

Helen：Please tell him to return my call.
請告訴他回我電話。

David：Does he know your phone number?
他知道妳的電話號碼嗎？

Helen：Yes, he has my phone number.
是的，他有我的電話號碼。

延伸用法

- He has company at this time.
  他現在有訪客。
- He's tied up at the moment.
  他現在正在忙。
- He's off today.
  他今天休假。
- He's on lunch.
  他正（外出）吃午餐。
- He's on lunch break.
  他在午休時間。
- He's out to lunch.
  他外出吃午餐。

相關用法

- I am sorry, but he's not at his desk now.
  很抱歉，他現在不在座位上。
- I am sorry, but he just went out.
  很抱歉，他剛出去。
- I am afraid he's not here.
  他恐怕不在這裡。

Unit 09 回電

I am returning your call.

我現在回你電話。

David : Hello?

哈囉？

Maria : Hi, David, this is Maria.

嗨，大衛，我是瑪麗亞。

David : Hi, Maria. What's up?

嗨，瑪麗亞。有事嗎？

Maria : I am returning your call.

我現在回你電話。

David : Oh, yeah. Look, I'm kind of busy now.

喔，對。聽著，我現在有一點忙。

Maria : No problem. Call me when you are available.

沒問題的。等你有空再打電話給我。

David : I'll. Bye.

我會的。再見。

延伸用法

- I was just about to call you.
  我剛好要打電話給你。

- You called me last night, didn't you?
  你昨晚打電話給我，不是嗎？

- Thank you for returning my call.
  謝謝你回我電話。

- That's all right. I'll try to call him later.
  沒關係。我晚一點再打電話給他。

- I'll try again later.
  我晚一點再試一次（打電話）。

- I'll return his call.
  我會回他的電話。

相關用法

- When should I call back then?
  那我應該什麼時候回電？

- Can I call again in 10 minutes?
  我可以十分鐘後再打電話過來嗎？

- Would you tell him I called?
  你能告訴他我來電過嗎？

Unit 10 轉接電話

I'll put you through.

我幫你轉接過去。

David : Could you put me through to
John, please?

能幫我轉接電話給約翰嗎？

Helen : Who is calling, please?

請問你的大名？

David : This is David Jones.

我是大衛‧瓊斯。

Helen : OK, Mr. Jones, I'll put you
through.

好的，瓊斯先生，我會幫你轉接過去。

David : Thank you.

謝謝你。

Helen : You are welcome. Hold on a
second, please.

不客氣。請稍候。

延伸用法

- I'll transfer your call.
  我會幫你轉接電話。
- I'll connect you.
  我會幫你轉接電話。
- I'm transferring your call.
  我幫你轉接電話。
- I'm redirecting your call.
  我幫你轉接電話。
- I'm connecting you now.
  我現在就幫你轉接電話過去。

相關用法

- I'll put him on.
  我把電話轉給他。
- I'll transfer your call to Mr. Jones.
  我會幫你轉接給瓊斯先生。
- I'll connect you to extension 747.
  我幫你轉到分機747。

Unit 11 詢問來電者身分

Who is this?

您是哪位？

Helen: Hello?

哈囉？

David: May I talk to your manager?

我能不能跟你們經理講話？

Helen: Who is this?

您是哪位？

David: This is David Jones.

我是大衛‧瓊斯。

Helen: I'll put him on.

我把電話轉給他。

（稍後）

David: Mr. White?

懷特先生嗎？

Mr. White: Keep going.

說吧！

延伸用法

- May I ask who is calling?
  請問您是哪位？
- May I know who is calling?
  請問您的大名？
- Who is calling, please?
  請問您的大名？
- Whom I'm speaking with?
  我正在跟誰講話呢？
- Who should I say is calling?
  我要說是誰來電？
- May I have your name, please?
  請問您的大名？

相關用法

- And you are?
  您是？
- Are you Mr. Jones?
  您是瓊斯先生嗎？
- You are...?
  您是…？

Unit 12 接受電話留言

May I take a message?

要我記下留言嗎？

Helen：May I speak to Chris, please?
我能和克里斯說話嗎？

David：He's on another line.
他正忙線中。

Helen：May I take a message?
要我記下留言嗎？

David：How about Bob? Could I talk to him?
那鮑勃呢？我能和他說話嗎？

Helen：I'm sorry but there's no Bob in this office. May I take a message?
抱歉，我們公司沒有叫鮑勃的人。要我記下留言嗎？

David：Sure. Tell Chris to fax me the quotation, please.
好的。請告訴克里斯傳真報價單給我。

延伸用法

- Let me take a message.

  我來(幫您)記下留言。

- What do you want me to tell him?

  要我轉達什麼給他嗎？

- Would you like to leave a message?

  你要留言嗎？

- Do you have any message?

  你有要留言嗎？

- Is there any message?

  有沒有要留言？

- Let me write down your message.

  我來寫下你的留言。

相關用法

- Do you want him to return your call?

  你要他回你電話嗎？

- Does he have your number?

  他知道你的號碼嗎？

- How can he get a hold of you?

  他要怎麼和你聯絡？

Unit 13 請對方代為轉告

Could I leave him a message?

我能留言給他嗎？

Helen : Hello, may I speak to Chris?

哈囉，我能和克里斯説話嗎？

David : He's on another line.

他正忙線中。

Helen : Could I leave him a message?

我能留言給他嗎？

David : Sure.

好的。

Helen : Please ask him to call me back.

請告訴他回我電話。

David : OK, I'll have him call you back.

好的，我會請他回妳電話。

Helen : Thank you so much.

非常感謝！

David : You're welcome.

不客氣。

延伸用法

- Would you tell Mr. Jones David called, please?
  能請你告訴瓊斯先生，大衛打過電話嗎？
- Would you ask him to call Mark at 8647-3663?
  你能請他打電話到 8647-3663 給馬克嗎？
- Call me at 8647-3663, extension 747, after three pm.
  下午三點以後，打電話到 8647-3663 分機 747 給我。

相關用法

- Tell him to give me a call as soon as possible.
  告訴他盡快回我電話。
- Please tell him to return my call.
  請告訴他回我電話。
- My number is 8647-3663.
  我的號碼是 8647-3663。

Unit 14 打錯電話

You must have the wrong
number.

你一定是打錯電話了。

Helen : May I speak to Chris, please?
我能和克里斯說話嗎？

David : Who are you trying to reach?
妳找哪位呀？

Helen : Chris White.
克里斯・懷特。

David : You must have the wrong number.
妳一定是打錯電話了。

Helen : Is this 8647-3663?
這裡是 8647-3663 嗎？

David : Yes, but there is no one here by
that name.
是啊，但這裡沒有這個人。

Helen : Oh, sorry for troubling you.
哦，對不起打擾你了。

延伸用法

- I'm afraid you've got the wrong number.
  你恐怕撥錯電話了。
- You must dial the wrong number.
  你一定撥錯電話號碼了。
- What number are you dialing?
  你打幾號？
- What number are you trying to reach?
  你打幾號？
- There is no one here by that name.
  這裡沒有這個人。
- There is no David here.
  這裡沒有大衛這個人。

相關用法

- Did I have the wrong number?
  我打錯電話號碼了嗎？
- I'm calling 8647-3663.
  我撥的電話是 8647-3663。
- Is this 8647-3663?
  這是 8647-3663 嗎？

Unit 15 電話中聽不清楚

Could you repeat that, please?

能請你再說一遍嗎？

David : Hello, may I speak to Chris now?
哈囉，我現在能和克里斯說話嗎？

Susan : I'm sorry, but he's still on the phone.
抱歉，但是他還在講電話。

David : When will he get off the phone?
他什麼時候會講完電話？

Susan : I'm not sure. Shall I take a message?
我不確定。要不要我幫你留言？

David : Tell him to call David back if possible.
告訴他，如果可能的話回電給大衛。

Susan : Could you repeat that, please?
能請你再說一遍嗎？

David : Tell him to call David Jones back.
告訴他回電給大衛‧瓊斯。

Susan : I'll.
我會的。

延伸用法

- Pardon?

  你説什麼？

- What did you just say?

  你剛剛説什麼？

- What? I can't hear you.

  什麼？我聽不見你説什麼。

- I can't hear you very well.

  我聽不清楚你説什麼。

- Could you speak up a little, please?

  能請你説大聲一點嗎？

- Speak up a little, please.

  請説大聲一點！

相關用法

- Hello? Anybody there?

  哈囉？有人在聽嗎？

- I think that the lines are crossed or something.

  我想線路可能有干擾或有問題。

Unit 16 電話禮儀

I hope I didn't disturb you.

我希望我沒有打擾你。

David : Hello?

哈囉?

Susan : David? This is Susan.

大衛嗎?我是蘇珊。

David : Hi, Susan. How are you doing?

嗨,蘇珊,妳好嗎?

Susan : I'm fine. Listen, David, I hope I didn't disturb you.

我很好。大衛,聽著,希望我沒有打擾到你。

David : No, not at all. What's up?

沒有,完全不會。有事嗎?

Susan : I'm calling to ask you a question.

我打電話來問你一個問題。

David : Keep going.

請說。

延伸用法

- I am sorry to call you so late.
  我很抱歉這麼晚打電話給你。
- Did I disturb you?
  我有打擾到你嗎？
- Am I calling at a bad time?
  我打來得不是時候嗎？
- Hi, Barry. Got a minute now?
  嗨，貝瑞，現在有空嗎？
- Could you spell your name, please?
  能請您拼一遍您的名字嗎？
- Please give me the phone number of Mr. Kim.
  請給我金先生的電話號碼。

相關用法

- Let me check it for you.
  我來幫你確認。
- Have a good day.
  祝你有美好的一天。

Unit 17 打電話遇到困難

Your line is always engaged.

你的電話一直佔線中。

David : Did anybody called today?
今天有人打電話來嗎？

Helen : Yes. Your boss called this afternoon.
有啊。你老闆今天下午有打電話來。

David : What did he say?
他有說什麼嗎？

Helen : I'm not sure. The lines were crossed.
我不確定。電話有干擾。

David : Did he try again?
他有再打嗎？

Helen : No. It seems that he complained your line was always engaged.
沒有。好像是他抱怨你的電話一直在佔線中。

David : That's OK. I'll call him back tomorrow.
沒關係。我明天會回電話給他。

延伸用法

- My call didn't go through.
  我的電話並沒有撥通。
- The phone isn't working.
  電話故障了。
- The line is busy.
  忙線中。
- It's making a funny noise.
  （電話）它發出怪聲音。
- We have a bad connection.
  我們的線路不太順。

相關用法

- The lines are crossed.
  電話有干擾。
- The phone went dead.
  電話不通了。
- This is a really bad line.
  電話線路有問題。

Unit 18 結束通話

I'd better get going.

我要掛電話了。

David : So you are saying that we should accept his offer?

所以你是説我們應該接受他的提議囉？

Helen : Maybe it's a good chance, right?

也許這是個好機會，對吧？

David : Of course. Look, it's pretty late now.

當然。聽著，現在很晚了。

Helen : I guess I'd better get going.

我想我要掛電話了。

David : OK. Let's talk it over tomorrow. See you tomorrow.

好。明天再討論吧！明天見囉！

Helen : Bye.

拜！

延伸用法

- I've got to hang up the phone.
  我要掛電話了。
- I'd better get off the phone.
  我必須掛電話了。
- I've got to hang up the phone now.
  我現在要掛電話了。
- I've got to leave now.
  我現在要掛電話了。
- Nice talking to you.
  很高興和你說話。

相關用法

- Thank you for calling.
  謝謝你打電話來。
- You can call me anytime.
  歡迎隨時打電話給我。
- Just give me a call when you have a chance.
  只要有空就打電話給我吧。

Unit 01 只看不買

I'm just looking.

我只是隨便看看。

David: How late are you open?
你們營業到幾點？

Maria: We are open until eight thirty.
我們營業到八點卅分。

David: I see.
我瞭解。

Maria: May I help you with something?
需要我的幫忙嗎？

David: No. I'm just looking.
不用。我只是隨便看看。

Maria: Take your time. If you need any help, just let me know. My name is Maria.
您慢慢看。假如您需要任何幫忙，讓我知道就好。我叫做瑪莉亞。

David: Sure.
好的。

① ③ ①
1 生活常用
2 辦公室
3 電話
4 購物
5 人際關係
6 客套短語
7 交通
8 問路

延伸用法

- No. Thanks.
  不用。謝謝！
- Maybe later. Thank you.
  也許等一下。謝謝。
- I don't need any help.
  我不需要任何服務。
- Not yet. Thanks.
  還不需要。謝謝！

Unit 02 對商品有興趣

I'm interested in those gloves.

我對那一些手套有興趣。

Maria : What would you like to see?
您想看些什麼？

David : I'm interested in those gloves.
我對那一些手套有興趣。

Maria : Is it a present for someone?
是送給誰的禮物嗎？

David : Yes, it's for my daughter.
是的，是給我女兒的。

Maria : Is there anything special in your mind?
在你的心裡有想好要什麼嗎？

David : I need a pair of red gloves.
我需要一雙紅色的手套。

Maria : Sorry, I'm all out of red ones.
抱歉，我紅色的都缺貨。

0 3 3

1 生活常用

2 辦公室

3 電話

4 購物

5 人際關係

6 寒喧短語

7 交通

8 問路

延伸用法

- I need to buy birthday presents for my wife.

  我需要幫我太太買生日禮物。

- I'm looking for some gifts for my daughter.

  我在找一些要送給我女兒的禮物。

- Is there any souvenirs made in the USA?

  有沒有美國製造的紀念品?

- I want to buy the earrings.

  我想要買耳環。

- I'm looking for some skirts.

  我正在找一些裙子。

相關用法

- Do you have any purple hats?

  你們有紫色的帽子嗎?

- Do you have any red ones?

  你們有紅色的嗎?

Unit 03 選購商品

I'd like to see some ties.

我想看一些領帶。

Maria : What would you like to see?
您想看些什麼？

David : I'd like to see some blue ties.
我想看一些藍色的領帶。

Maria : I don't have any more blue ones. I just have yellow ones.
我沒有藍色的。我只有一些黃色的。

David : I'd likc to take a look.
我想要看一下。

Maria : Sure. How do you like them?
好啊！您喜歡他們嗎？

David : They are great. By the way, do you have any hats?
他們很不錯。還有，你們有賣帽子嗎？

Maria : Let me show you some elegant hats.
我給您看一些很雅致的帽子。

1 3 5

1 生活常用

2 辦公室

3 電話

4 購物

5 人際關係

6 客套短語

7 交通

8 問路

延伸用法

- I'm interested in this computer.
  我對這台電腦有興趣。
- May I see those MP3 players?
  我能看那些MP3播放器嗎?
- May I have a look at them?
  我能看一看它們嗎?
- Can you show me something different?
  您能給我看一些不一樣的嗎?

相關用法

- Show me that pen.
  給我看那支筆。

Unit 04 參觀中意商品

Show me that black sweater.

給我看看那件黑色毛衣。

Maria : Did you find something you like?
有找到您喜歡的東西了嗎?

David : They look nice.
他們看起來都不錯。

Maria : Which one do you like?
您喜歡哪一件?

David : Show me that black sweater.
給我看看那件黑色毛衣。

Maria : Is this what you are looking for?
您要找的是這一種嗎?

David : No, I don't like this one.
不要,我不喜歡這一件。

Maria : How about this red one?
那這個紅色的呢?

David : Yes, I want this one.
是的,我要這一種。

1
3
7

1 生活常用
2 辦公室
3 電話
4 購物
5 人際關係
6 客套短語
7 交通
8 問路

延伸用法

- Those skirts look great.
  那些裙子看起來不錯。
- That one on the bottom shelf.
  在底層架子上的那一件。
- Do you have any hats like this one?
  你們有沒有像這類的帽子？
- Do you have anything better?
  你們有沒有好一點的？
- Is that all?
  全部就這些嗎？
- Anything else?
  還有其他的嗎？

相關用法

- No, thanks.
  不用，謝謝！
- It's not what I need.
  這不是我需要的。
- It's not what I'm looking for.
  我不是要找這一種。

Unit 05 特定商品

I'd like to buy some gloves.

我想要買一些手套。

Maria : Looking for anything special?
要找特定的東西嗎？

David : They are suitable for my daughters.
他們是很適合我的女兒們。

Maria : What do you want to buy?
您想買什麼？

David : I'd like to buy some gloves.
我想要買一些手套。

Maria : Do you also need a scarf?
您也需要圍巾嗎？

David : Yes, I want to take a look.
是的，我想要看一看。

Maria : Anything else?
還有要看其他東西嗎？

David : That's all.
就這些。

1 生活常用
2 辦公室
3 電話
4 購物
5 人際關係
6 客套短語
7 交通
8 問路

延伸用法

- Do you have any onion?
  你們有賣洋蔥嗎？
- I'd like some pears too.
  我也要買一些梨子。
- I need some apples.
  我需要一些蘋果。

Unit 06 商品的功能

What's this for?

這是做什麼用的？

Maria : Could you show me how it works?
你可以展示給我看怎麼操作嗎？

David : Yes, of course.
好的，當然可以。

Maria : What's this for?
這是做什麼用的？

David : It's a bag.
它是個袋子。

Maria : Really?
真的？

David : Let me show you. See? You can store it like this.
我展示給你看。看見了嗎？你可以像這樣收放這個東西。

Maria : I see. Thank you.
我瞭解了。謝謝你。

1 生活常用 2 辦公室 3 電話 4 購物 5 人際關係 6 客套短語 7 交通 8 問路

延伸用法

- What's this?

  這是什麼？

- What's this thing for?

  這東西是做什麼用的？

- How do you use it?

  你是如何使用的？

- How do you operate it?

  你是如何操作的？

- Is it hard to use it?

  會很難使用嗎？

相關用法

- Please show me again.

  請再表演一次給我看。

- Amazing.

  真是神奇。

Unit 07 特定顏色

Do you have any ones in pink?

你們有粉紅色的嗎？

Maria: They are new arrivals.
他們都是新品。

David: Can I pick it up?
我可以拿起來(看看)嗎？

Maria: Yes, please. Red is in fashion.
好的，請便。紅色正在流行。

David: Well, I don't think my wife would like this color.
嗯，我不這麼認為我太太會喜歡這個顏色。

Maria: What color do you like?
您想要哪一個顏色？

David: Do you have any ones in pink?
你們有粉紅色的嗎？

Maria: We only have red ones.
我們只有紅色的。

1 生活常用
2 辦公室
3 電話
4 購物
5 人際關係
6 客套短語
7 交通
8 問路

延伸用法

- I'd prefer the blue ones.
  我偏好藍色的這些。
- I'm looking for the black socks.
  我在找黑色的襪子。
- Both red and pink are OK.
  紅色或粉紅色都可以。
- Do you have this size in any other colors?
  有這個尺寸的其他顏色嗎？

相關用法

- Let me take some blue skirts for you.
  讓我拿一些藍色裙子給您。
- How about this one?
  這一個如何？
- How about this color?
  這個顏色如何？

Unit 08 尺寸

My size is 8.

我的尺寸是八號。

Maria: This comes in several sizes.
這有好多種尺寸。

David: What sizes do you have?
你們有什麼尺寸？

Maria: What size do you wear — a twelve?
您穿幾號，12 號嗎？

David: My size is twelve or fourteen.
我的尺寸是 12 號或 14 號。

Maria: I can measure you up.
我可以幫您量。

David: Thanks.
謝謝！

Maria: Your size is fourteen.
您的尺寸是 14 號。

David: The fourteens are over there.
14 號的都在那裡。

①
④
⑤

① 生活常用

② 辦公室

③ 電話

④ 購物

⑤ 人際關係

⑥ 客套短語

⑦ 交通

⑧ 問路

延伸用法

- Any other sizes?
  有沒有其他尺寸？
- I don't know my size.
  我不知道我的尺寸。
- My size is between 8 and 7.
  我的尺寸是介於8號和7號之間。
- I want the large size.
  我要大尺寸的。
- It's a small and I wear a medium.
  這是小號的，而我穿中號的。
- Do you have this one in small size?
  你們有這一種小號的嗎？

相關用法

- Medium, please.
  請給我中號。
- Give me size 8.
  給我8號。
- Size 8 in black.
  (給我)黑色的8號尺寸。

Unit 09 不中意商品

I don't like this style.

我不喜歡這個款式。

Maria : We have some nice ones on sale.
我們有一些品質不錯的在特價中。

David : Where are they?
在哪裡？

Maria : What do you think of these?
這些您覺得如何呢？

David : I don't like this style.
我不喜歡這個款式。

Maria : How about this one?
那這個呢？

David : It seems a little old-fashioned.
好像有些老氣。

Maria : Sorry, that's all we have.
抱歉，我們只有這些。

延伸用法

- It's not the right size.
  尺寸不對。
- I don't want this style.
  我不想要這個款式。
- I don't prefer this kind of color.
  我不偏好這種顏色。
- I dislike this one.
  我不喜歡這一個。
- I hate this style.
  我討厭這個款式。

Unit 10 試穿衣服

Can I try this on?

我可以試穿這一件嗎？

Maria：Maybe you would like a blue shirt.

也許您想要一件藍色襯衫。

David：Great, I think that's what I want.

很好，我想這就是我要的。

Maria：Would you like to try it on?

您要試穿看看嗎？

David：OK.

好啊。

Cathy：Can I try this on too?

我也可以試穿這一件嗎？

James：Sure. This way please.

好啊。這邊請。

Maria：How about the size?

這個尺寸如何？

David：I should try another bigger one.

我應該要試穿另一件大一點的。

1
4
9

1 生活常用
2 辦公室
3 電話
4 購物
5 人際關係
6 客套短語
7 交通
8 問路

延伸用法

- I'll try on a small.
  我要試穿小號的。
- Can I try it on?
  我可以試穿嗎?
- May I try on that one too?
  我也可以試穿那一件嗎?
- I'd like to try this coat on and see if it fits.
  我想試穿這件外套,看看是否合身。
- Where is the fitting room?
  試衣間在哪裡?

相關用法

- I'm sorry, but it's not allowed to try it on.
  抱歉,不可以試穿。
- You can try this one.
  您可以試穿這一件。

Unit 11 試穿特定尺寸

Could I try a larger one?

我可以試穿大一點的嗎？

David: Would you show me something special?

可以給我看一些特別的嗎？

Maria: How about them? They look great together.

它們如何？它們搭配起來不錯。

David: Which one is better?

哪一件比較好？

Maria: Red is in fashion.

紅色正在流行。

David: I don't know what my size is.

我不知道我的尺寸。

Maria: It's size 32, right?

是 32 號，對嗎？

David: Could I try a larger one?

我可以試穿大一點的嗎？

1 生活常用

2 辦公室

3 電話

4 購物

5 人際關係

6 客套短語

7 交通

8 問路

Maria : Yes, please.
　　　　好的，沒問題。

延伸用法

● I'll try on size 8.
　我要試穿8號。

● Can I try a smaller one?
　我能試穿較小件的嗎？

● Do you have this color in size 8?
　這個顏色有8號的嗎？

● Do you have these shoes in size 7?
　這些鞋子你有7號的嗎？

● I need a fourteen.
　我需要14號。

相關用法

● This size is fine.
　這個尺寸可以。

● This is my size.
　這是我的尺寸。

Unit 12 試穿結果

How does this one look on me?

我穿這一件的效果怎麼樣?

David: How does this one look on me?
我穿這一件的效果怎麼樣?

Maria: It looks great on you.
您穿看起來不錯。

David: Where is the mirror? Well, I don't think so.
鏡子在哪裡?嗯,我不這麼認為。

Maria: But you look terrific.
但是您看起來真的不錯耶!

David: You think so? I have no idea.
妳這麼認為嗎?我拿不定主意。

Maria: Your clothes fit perfectly.
您的衣服十分合身。

David: But it's not very comfortable.
但是(穿起來)不舒服。

① 生活常用
② 辦公室
③ 電話
④ 購物
⑤ 人際關係
⑥ 客套短語
⑦ 交通
⑧ 問路

①⑤③

延伸用法

- It looks OK on me.

  我穿看起來不錯。

- It feels fine.

  感覺不錯。

- Not bad.

  不錯。

- It looks perfect to me.

  這個我喜歡。

- I don't think this is good.

  我不覺得這件好。

相關用法

- Don't you think it's too loose?

  你不覺得太寬鬆嗎？

- The waist was a little tight.

  腰部有一點緊。

Unit 13 樣式

Do you have anything like this one?

有沒有像這個的？

Maria : That's the style this year.
　　　　這是今年流行的款式。

David : Do you have anything like this one? More fashionable.
　　　　有沒有像這個的？流行一點的。

Maria : Yes. What color do you prefer? Black or brown?
　　　　有的。您偏好哪一種顏色？黑色或棕色？

David : I'm not sure. Let me take a look.
　　　　我不確定。讓我看一看。

Maria : OK, let me take one for you.
　　　　好的，讓我拿一件給您。

David : I can't tell the difference.
　　　　我看不出來有什麼差別。

1 生活常用
2 辦公室
3 電話
4 購物
5 人際關係
6 客套短語
7 交通
8 問路

延伸用法

- Any other colors?
  有沒有其他顏色？

- Any other styles?
  有沒有其他款式？

- Do you have plain ones?
  有沒有樸素一點的？

- I prefer conservative ones.
  我偏好保守一點的。

- That's the style this year, isn't it?
  這是今年的款式，對吧？

- Is this one different from that red one?
  這個和紅色那個不同嗎？

相關用法

- What's the difference between them?
  它們之間有什麼不同？

- What style would you like?
  您想要哪一種款式？

- The model A is new arrival.
  款式A是新貨。

Unit 14 售價

How much is this, please?

請問這個要多少錢？

1 生活常用

2 辦公室

3 電話

4 購物

5 人際關係

6 客套短語

7 交通

8 問路

David : Do you have this shirt in size 38?
這件襯衫有沒有 38 號？

Maria : Yes. Here you are.
有的。在這裡。

David : I like this one.
我喜歡這一件。

Maria : Our sale will be continuing until next week.
我們的特價只到下週。

David : Well, I've to think about it.
嗯，我要想一想。

Maria : That sweater's a great buy.
那件毛衣真的很划算。

David : How much is this, please?
請問這個要多少錢？

Maria : It's four hundred.
要四百(元)。

延伸用法

- How much?

  多少錢？

- How much is it?

  這個多少錢？

- How much are those apples?

  那些蘋果要多少錢？

- How much does it cost?

  這個要賣多少錢？

- How much did you say?

  你說要多少錢？

- What's the price for this camera?

  這台相機多少錢？

- How much is it together?

  總共多少錢？

相關用法

- How much shall I pay for it?

  這個我應該付多少錢？

- How much shall I pay for this one and that one?

  這一件和那一件我應該付多少錢？

Unit 15 售價太貴

It's too expensive.

它太貴了。

1 生活常用

2 辦公室

3 電話

4 購物

5 人際關係

6 客套短語

7 交通

8 問路

Maria : Can I show you anything else?
需要我給您看其他商品嗎？

David : Yes, please.
好啊，麻煩您了。

Maria : Here you are. It costs seven hundred dollars plus tax.
在這裡。它含稅要七千元。

David : Seven hundred dollars?
七千元？

Maria : What do you think of the price?
您覺得價格如何？

David : It's too expensive.
它太貴了。

Maria : I can give you a discount if you buy two sweaters.
如果你買兩件毛衣，我可以給你折扣。

延伸用法

- So expensive?

  這麼貴？

- Is it expensive?

  會很貴嗎？

- Don't you think it's too expensive?

  你不覺得太貴了嗎？

相關用法

- I can't afford it.

  我付不起。

① 生活常用

② 辦公室

③ 電話

④ 購物

⑤ 人際關係

⑥ 客套短語

⑦ 交通

⑧ 問路

Unit 16 討價還價

Can you lower the price?

你可以算便宜一點嗎？

David : How much are those watches?
那些錶多少錢？

Maria : The white ones or the golden ones?
白色或是金色的？

David : The golden ones.
金色的

Maria : Three thousand each.
每一支三千(元)。

David : Can you lower the price?
你可以算便宜一點嗎？

Maria : What price range are you looking for?
您想要多少錢？

David : Is there a discount for two?
買兩支可以有折扣吧？

Maria : How about a 10 percent discount?
打九折如何？

延伸用法

- Can you give me a 10 percent discount?
  您能給我九折嗎？

- Can you lower the price a bit if I buy them?
  如果我買它們，您可以算便宜一點嗎？

- Is there a discount for two?
  買兩件可以有折扣吧？

- Are there any discounts?
  有沒有折扣？

- Can you give me a discount?
  您可以給我折扣嗎？

- Can you make it cheaper?
  可以算便宜一點嗎？

相關用法

- Can you lower it two hundred?
  可以便宜兩百(元)嗎？

- How about five thousand dollars?
  可以算五千元嗎？

Unit 17 購買

I'll take the small ones.

我要買小的。

David : How much are the oranges?
那些柳橙要多少錢？

Maria : These?
這些嗎？

David : No, the small ones.
不是，是小的。

Maria : Oh, those. They are five for eighty.
喔，那些喔！他們是五個八十(元)。

David : And the large ones - how much are they?
那麼那些大的要多少錢？

Maria : Twenty dollars each.
每一個廿十元。

David : OK, I'll take the small ones.
好。我要買小的。

Maria : How many?
要多少個？

David : Five, please.
請給我五個。

❶ 生活常用
❷ 辦公室
❸ 電話
❹ 購物
❺ 人際關係
❻ 客套短語
❼ 交通
❽ 問路

延伸用法

- I'll take it.
  我要買它。
- I'll take those.
  我要買那些。
- I'll take these.
  我要買這些。
- I'll get this one.
  我要買這一件。
- I want both of them.
  它們兩個我都要。
- I want two of these.
  我要買這兩個。

相關用法

- No, I'll pass this time.
  不要,我這次不買。
- Not for this time.
  這次先不要(買)。
- I don't need any.
  我不需要。

Unit 18 付款

Cash, please.

用現金，麻煩你了。

David: I also need a pound of tomatoes.
我還要一磅的蕃茄。

Maria: OK. Anything else?
好的。還有要看其他的嗎？

David: No, that's all.
沒有，就這些。

Maria: Would you like some apples? I have some beautiful ones.
您要一些蘋果嗎？我有一些不錯的(蘋果)。

David: No, thanks. I don't need any.
不用，謝謝！我不需要。

Maria: OK. Let's see.... That would be two hundred dollars. How would you like to pay for it?
好的。我算算…。（總共）是兩百元。您要用什麼方式付款？

David: Cash, please.
用現金，麻煩你了。

延伸用法

- Credit card, please.
  用信用卡(付款)，麻煩你了。
- I'll pay it by cash.
  我要付現金。
- With traveler's check.
  用旅行支票(付款)。

相關用法

- Do you accept credit cards?
  你們接受信用卡付款嗎？
- Can I use VISA?
  我可以用VISA卡嗎？
- Do you take Master?
  你們接受萬事達卡嗎？

Unit 01 身體不舒服

I feel awful.

我覺得糟透了！

Helen : You really sound sick.
你聽起來生病了。

David : I feel awful.
我覺得糟透了！

Helen : What's the matter?
發生什麼事了？

David : My leg hurts.
我的腳好痛。

Helen : How do you feel now?
你現在覺得如何？

David : Not so good.
不太好。

Helen : Let me see.... It looks terrible.
You should stay in bed.
我看看…。看起來糟透了。你應該躺在床上的。

David : No. I'm going to see a doctor later.
不用。我等一下就要去看醫生。

1 生活常用
2 辦公室
3 電話
4 購物
5 人際關係
6 客套短語
7 交通
8 問路

延伸用法

- My throat hurts.
  我的喉嚨痛。
- My shoulder hurts.
  我的肩膀痛。
- I've got a headache.
  我頭痛。
- I've got a stomachache.
  我胃痛。
- I have a fever.
  我發燒了。
- I have the flu.
  我感冒了。

相關用法

- I'm not feeling well.
  我覺得不舒服。
- I don't feel well.
  我不舒服。
- I feel terrible.
  我感覺糟透了。

Unit 02 關心病人

You'd better get some rest.

你最好要多休息。

David: Ow!
噢！

Helen: Are you OK?
你還好吧？

David: Uh, I don't think so.
嗯，不太好。

Helen: What's the matter?
怎麼啦？

David: I sprained my ankle yesterday.
我昨天扭傷我的腳踝。

Helen: Did you see a doctor?
你有去看醫生嗎？

David: Yes, Jenny took me to the hospital.
有啊，珍妮有帶我去醫院。

Helen: You'd better get some rest.
你最好要多休息。

1
7
1

1 生活常用

2 辦公室

3 電話

4 購物

5 人際關係

6 客套短語

7 交通

8 問路

延伸用法

- You'd better go home.
  你最好回家。
- You need to lie down.
  你最好躺下。
- Try to get some sleep.
  試著睡覺吧！
- Stay in bed for a few days.
  在床上多躺躺休息幾天。
- Did you see a doctor?
  你有看醫生嗎？
- Did you take medicine?
  你有吃藥嗎？

相關用法

- Why don't you just go home?
  你怎麼不乾脆回家？
- Why don't you take some aspirin?
  你怎麼不吃些阿斯匹靈？

- Let me call an ambulance for you.
  讓我幫你叫救護車。

Unit 03 安撫情緒

I'm sorry to hear that.

我很遺憾聽見這件事。

Helen : Oh, my God.
噢！天啊！

David : What happened?
怎麼啦？

Helen : My mom just called. Kiki is dead.
我媽媽剛剛來電，Kiki 死了。

David : How did it happen?
怎麼發生的？

Helen : It's a car accident. Kiki was my best friend when I was a little girl.
是車禍。當我是小女孩時，Kiki 是我最要好的朋友。

David : I'm sorry to hear that.
我很遺憾聽見這件事。

1
7
3

1 生活常用

2 辦公室

3 電話

4 購物

5 人際關係

6 客套短語

7 交通

8 問路

延伸用法

- Come on.
  不要這樣。
- Give me a hug.
  給我一個擁抱。
- Don't worry about it.
  不要擔心。
- Everything will be fine.
  凡事都會沒問題的。
- I'm here with you.
  我在這裡陪你。
- You'll get through it.
  你會度過難關的。

相關用法

- It's not easy for you.
  難為你了。
- God bless you.
  上帝會保佑你。
- Take it easy.
  放輕鬆。

Unit 04 不要生氣

Don't be so mad.

不要這麼生氣。

1 生活常用

2 辦公室

3 電話

4 購物

5 人際關係

6 客套短語

7 交通

8 問路

Helen: Damn it!
可惡！

David: What's wrong?
怎麼啦？

Helen: Mark is seeing someone else.
馬克正在和某人約會。

David: I'm sorry to hear that.
我很抱歉聽見這件事。

Helen: How could he do this to me?
他怎麼能這麼對我？

David: I thought you were broken up.
我以為你們分手了。

Helen: That's right. But I still love him.
沒錯。可是我還是很愛他啊！

David: Come on, don't be so mad.
好了啦，不要這麼生氣。

延伸用法

- Don't be so angry.
  不要這麼生氣。
- It doesn't help.
  沒有幫助的。
- It's not your fault.
  不是你的錯。
- What a let down!
  真令人失望！
- That's going too far!
  這太離譜了！
- It's his lost.
  這是他的損失。

相關用法

- Calm down.
  冷靜點。
- Forget it.
  算了。
- Just let it be.
  算了吧！

① 生活常用

② 辦公室

③ 電話

④ 購物

⑤ 人際關係

⑥ 客套短語

⑦ 交通

⑧ 問路

Unit 05 勸人冷靜

Calm down.

冷靜點。

Helen: Oh, my God.
喔，我的天啊！

David: Something wrong?
怎麼啦？

Helen: You're not going to believe it.
你不會會相信這件事的。

David: Tell me.
說說看！

Helen: Mark has taken up with a married woman.
馬克和有夫之婦有染。

David: Really?
真的？

Helen: He is a cruel person.
他真是惡毒的人。

David: Calm down.
冷靜點。

延伸用法

- Don't panic.

  不要慌張。

- Don't lose your mind.

  不要失去理智。

- Don't worry about it.

  不要擔心。

- Don't take it so hard.

  看開一點。

- Just relax.

  放輕鬆。

- Just tell me what happened.

  告訴我發生什麼事了。

相關用法

- Do something.

  想想辦法。

- It's impossible.

  不可能。

- Take it easy for a while.

  稍微放輕鬆一下。

❶ 生活常用

❷ 辦公室

❸ 電話

❹ 購物

❺ 人際關係

❻ 客套短語

❼ 交通

❽ 問路

Unit 06 遭遇問題

You'd better report it to the police right away.

你最好馬上向警察報案。

David: I've got a fever and a really bad headache.

我發燒而且頭很痛。

Helen: Why don't you take some aspirin?

你為什麼不吃一些斯匹靈？

David: I've already tried that. But it didn't help.

我有試過。但是沒有幫助。

Helen: If I were you, I'd just lie down.

如果我是你，我就會躺下來。

David: But I can't.

但是我不能。

Helen: Why not?

為什麼不可以？

David: Because I just lost my passport.

因為我才剛遺失我的護照。

Helen: You'd better report it to the police right away.

你最好馬上向警察報案。

延伸用法

- You'd better call the bank immediately.

  你最好立刻通報銀行。

- You'd better take a vacation.

  你最好休假。

- You should eat somethimg.

  你應該吃點東西。

- You really ought to move out.

  你真的應該搬出去。

- You shouldn't work so hard.

  你不應該工作得這麼辛苦。

相關用法

- What I would do is call the police.

  我會做的是打電話報警。

- What I would do is go by bus.

  我會做的是搭公車去。

Unit 07 解決的辦法

Aren't you going to do something?

你不想辦法嗎？

David：Have you contacted Mr. Nelson yet?
妳聯絡尼爾森先生了嗎？

Jenny：No, not yet.
沒有，還沒有。

David：Why not? What's the matter?
為什麼沒有？發生什麼事了？

Jenny：I don't know his phone number.
我不知道他的電話號碼。

David：Aren't you going to do something?
妳不想辦法嗎？

Jenny：What should I do now?
我現在應該做什麼？

David：Well, find out his phone number and please contact him right away.
嗯，查出他的電話號碼，並請立即和他聯絡。

延伸用法

- Do you best.

  你要盡力。

- Use your head.

  動動腦想一想。

- You try to figure it out.

  你設著想辦法解決。

- Find your own way.

  用你自己的方法。

- It's your decision.

  這是你的決定。

- It's your responsibility.

  這是你的責任。

相關用法

- Why don't you try to do it?

  你為什麼不試著做這件事？

- Take my advice.

  聽我的建議。

- Try again.

  再試一次。

Unit 08 提出建議

Why don't we go out and do something?

我們何不出去找點事做？

David: You look upset.
妳看起來很沮喪喔！

Helen: I'm really in a bad mood today.
我今天心情真的不好。

David: Why?
為什麼？

Helen: I failed my exam.
我考試考砸了！

David: Come on. Don't worry about it.
不要這樣。不用擔心啦！

Helen: But...
可是…

David: Look, why don't we go out and do something?
聽我說，我們何不出去找點事做？

Helen: I don't think so.
我不這麼認為！（我不想去）

1 生活常用
2 辦公室
3 電話
4 購物
5 人際關係
6 客套短語
7 交通
8 問路

延伸用法

- Why don't we go out for dinner?
  我們何不出去吃晚餐？

- Why don't we go for a walk?
  我們何不出去走走？

- Why don't we go for a drive?
  我們何不開車出去兜兜風？

- How about hanging out with me?
  要不要和我出去晃晃？

- How do you like going to a concert?
  你要不要去聽演唱會？

- Maybe we can go to a movie.
  也許我們可以去看電影。

相關用法

- Do you want to go to a movie?
  你想去看電影嗎？

- Would you like to join me?
  要不要一起去？

- Come on. That would be fun.
  來嘛！會很好玩的。

Unit 09 當和事佬

He didn't mean it.

他不是故意的。

David: I won't forgive Tom.
我不會原諒湯姆。

Helen: What did he do?
他做了什麼事？

David: He tried to break into my house.
他試著要闖進我家。

Helen: So what? He's just a kid.
那又怎麼樣？他只不過是個孩子。

David: But he was so rude.
但是他很無禮啊！

Helen: He didn't mean it.
他不是故意的。

David: Well, what can I say? He's your son.
這個嘛，我能說什麼？他是妳的兒子。

延伸用法

● Please forgive him.

請原諒他。

● It's not what you thought.

事情不是你所想像的那樣。

● It's an accident.

這是個意外。

● It's my fault.

都是我的錯。

● You can't be serious.

你不是當真的吧！

相關用法

● You are missing my point.

你誤會我了。

● You have my word.

我向你保證。

Unit 10 詢問意見

What shall I do?

我應該怎麼做？

Jenny：What shall I do?
我應該怎麼做？

David：Do what you have to do.
做妳應該做的事。

Jenny：Should I tell Tracy about this?
我應該要告訴崔西這件事嗎？

David：It's up to you.
由妳決定。

Jenny：Maybe I should call her.
也許我應該打電話給她。

David：It's what I meant.
我就是這個意思。

Jenny：You are telling me.
還用你說。

1 生活常用
2 辦公室
3 電話
4 購物
5 人際關係
6 客套短語
7 交通
8 問路

延伸用法

- It really makes me confused.
  它讓我真的很困擾。
- I don't know what to do.
  我不知道要怎麼做。
- I'll try.
  我會試著做。
- I'll do my best.
  我會盡力。
- What do you think?
  你覺得呢？

相關用法

- I have an idea.
  我有一個主意。
- It'll all work out.
  事情會解決的。
- It's worth a shot.
  那值得一試。

Unit 11 瞭解對方

Oh, I see.

喔，我瞭解了。

David: Listen, can we give my sister a ride home tonight?
聽著，今晚我們可以順便讓我的姊妹搭便車嗎？

Jason: Sure. Uh...is Susan seeing some one now?
當然好。嗯…蘇珊現在有交往的對象嗎？

David: Susan? No, not at all.
蘇珊？沒有，完全沒有。

Jason: What do you think if I ask her out this weekend?
如果我這個週末約她出去，你覺得如何？

David: Susan and you? Oh, I see.
蘇珊和你？喔，我瞭解了。

延伸用法

- I understand.

  我理解。

- I know what you meant.

  我瞭解你的意思。

- Are you serious?

  你是認真的？

- Come again?

  你再說一次？

相關用法

- I think so.

  我是這麼認為。

- What's your point?

  你的重點是什麼？

Unit 12　談論天氣

It's really hot.

真的很熱！

David : I'm back.
　　　　我回來了。

Jenny : How is your date?
　　　　你的約會如何啦？

David : Not bad.
　　　　不錯。

Jenny : How is everything coming?
　　　　事情都還好吧？

David : Oh, fine. I answered a few letters.
　　　　What's the weather like out there?
　　　　喔，不錯。我回了幾封信。外面的天氣
　　　　如何？

Jenny : Terrible. It's really hot.
　　　　糟糕。真的很熱！

1 生活常用
2 辦公室
3 電話
4 購物
5 人際關係
6 客套短語
7 交通
8 問路

延伸用法

- It's cold.

  很冷。

- It's raining really hard.

  雨下得很大。

- It's a beautiful day.

  今天天氣很好。

- It's freezing.

  外面很冷。

- It's too windy.

  風太大了。

- It's burning up out there.

  外面熱得跟火爐似的。

相關用法

- We had a downpour.

  我們剛遇到了一場傾盆大雨。

- Is it supposed to rain on Monday?

  星期一有可能會下雨嗎？

- What's the weather going to be like?

  天氣會如何？

Unit 13 談論家人

Do you have any children?

你有小孩嗎？

David: Do you have any children?

你有小孩嗎？

Helen: Yes, I do. I have a little boy and a little girl.

有的，我有。我有一個小男孩和一個小女孩。

David: How old are they?

他們多大年紀？

Helen: My son Jeff is six, and Kate is three. Here is their picture.

我兒子傑夫六歲，而凱特三歲。這是他們的照片。

David: They are adorable.

他們好可愛！

Helen: Yes, they are.

是啊，他們是(好可愛)。

1 生活常用

2 辦公室

3 電話

4 購物

5 人際關係

6 客套短語

7 交通

8 問路

延伸用法

- Do you have any kids?

  你有小孩嗎？

- Do you have any brothers or sisters?

  你有兄弟姊妹嗎？

- How old is your son?

  你兒子幾歲？

- How old is your baby?

  你的寶貝幾歲？

- How old is your little girl?

  你的小女兒幾歲？

相關用法

- How many kids do you have?

  你有多少小孩？

- How many siblings do you have?

  你有多少兄弟姊妹？

- Do you live with your parents?

  你和父母一起住嗎？

Unit 14 談論興趣

Are you going jogging?

你要去慢跑嗎?

David: Are you going jogging, Chris?
克里斯,你要去慢跑嗎?

Chris: No, I've got a basketball game tonight.
不要。我今晚有場籃球賽。

David: Oh, really? Do you play on a team?
喔,真的?你有參加隊伍(打籃球)嗎?

Chris: Yeah, I'm on a team in the Taiwan University.
是啊,我有參加台灣大學的隊伍。

David: Really? So do I.
真的?我也是。

Chris: Do you like football?
你喜歡橄欖球嗎?

David: I'm not crazy about it.
我不熱衷。

Chris: No, neither am I.
嗯,我也不熱衷。

1 生活常用
2 辦公室
3 電話
4 購物
5 人際關係
6 客套短語
7 交通
8 問路

延伸用法

- My favorite sport is swimming.
  我最喜歡的運動是游泳。
- I like to climb mountains on weekend.
  我喜歡在週末爬山。
- I watch basketball on TV.
  我看電視籃球賽。
- I love sailing.
  我喜歡航海。
- I play tennis every week.
  我每個星期都有打網球。
- Do you like jazz?
  你喜歡爵士樂嗎？

相關用法

- I'm interesting in baseball game.
  我對棒球有興趣。
- I'm not interested in sports.
  我對運動沒興趣。
- I'm not too interested in sports.
  我對運動不太有興趣。

Unit 15 建立交情

Can I get you anything?

要我幫你帶什麼嗎?

David: Oh, I'm really tired.
唷,我好累!

Helen: Me too.
我也是。

David: Where can I get a cup of coffee around here?
這附近哪裡有賣咖啡?

Helen: There is a coffee shop on the corner.
街角有一間咖啡館。

David: Can I get you anything?
要我幫妳帶什麼嗎?

Helen: Uh...could you bring me a Cappuccino?
嗯…你可以幫我帶一杯卡布其諾嗎?

David: Sure.
好啊!

197
1 生活常用
2 辦公室
3 電話
4 購物
5 人際關係
6 客套短語
7 交通
8 問路

延伸用法

- What do you want?

  你要什麼？

- What would you like?

  你要什麼？

- How about you?

  你呢？

- Just let me know.

  只要讓我知道就好。

- I could do it for you.

  我可以幫你。

相關用法

- I can help you.

  我可以幫你。

- How can I help you?

  我要怎麼幫你？

- You can count on me.

  你可以依賴我。

Unit 16 提出邀請

Do you want to come along?

你要一起來嗎？

David: Hey, Chris, how are you doing? We are going out for pizza tonight. Do you want to come along?

嗨，克里斯，你好嗎？我們今晚要去吃披薩。你要一起來嗎？

Chris: I'd really like to, but I have to ask my parents.

我真的很想去，但是我要問問我的父母。

David: Well, call me when you get home.

嗯，你到家的時候打電話給我。

Chris: Hey, David, there's Jason.

嘿，大衛，杰生在那裡。

David: Hmm...maybe he'd like to come with you tonight.

嗯，也許他今晚可以和你們一起去。

199

1 生活常用
2 辦公室
3 電話
4 購物
5 人際關係
6 客套短語
7 交通
8 問路

延伸用法

- Do you want to come over?
  你(們)要來嗎?
- Would you like to join us?
  你(們)要加入我們嗎?
- Would you like to see a movie?
  你(們)要看電影嗎?
- Would you like to come to my party?
  你(們)要不要參加我的宴會?
- I was wondering if you'd like to go to the movies.
  我在想,你(們)要不要去看電影?

相關用法

- How about having dinner with me?
  要和我一起吃晚餐嗎?
- Do you want to go out for dinner tonight?
  今晚要一起出去吃晚餐嗎?
- How about I pick you up at your place at 7?
  我七點去你家接你好嗎?

Unit 17 值得慶祝

Let's really celebrate.

我們來慶祝一下。

David : Hi, Jason.

嗨,杰生。

Jason : Hi, David. How was your day?

嗨,大衛。你好嗎?

David : Pretty good. Guess what? I've found a job.

還不錯。你知道嗎?我找到工作了。

Jason : Congratulations. Let's really celebrate.

恭喜你!我們來慶祝一下。

David : Sure. Why don't we go out to dinner? I'll treat.

當然好。我們何不出去吃晚餐?我請客。

Jason : OK. Let's go.

好啊!我們走!

2
0
1

1 生活常用

2 辦公室

3 電話

4 購物

5 人際關係

6 客套短語

7 交通

8 問路

延伸用法

- Maybe we should celebrate it.
  也許我們應該要慶祝一下。
- Let's go for a drink.
  我們去喝一杯。
- It sounds great.
  聽起來不錯。

相關用法

- Good for you.
  對你來說很好。
- I'm glad for you.
  我為你感到高興。

Unit 18 小道消息

Did you hear what happened?

你有聽說發生什麼事了嗎？

Jenny : Did you hear what happened?
你有聽說發生什麼事了嗎？

David : No.
沒有。

Jenny : Maria and Jason are in hospital.
瑪麗亞和杰生住院了。

David : Why? What happened to them?
為什麼？他們怎麼啦？

Jenny : They had a terrible fight yesterday.
他們昨天嚴重地打了一架。

David : My God.
我的天啊！

Jenny : Don't worry about them. They'll be fine.
不用擔心他們。他們沒事的。

David : I hope so.
我希望是如此。

延伸用法

● Did you know that thing?
　你知道那件事了嗎？

● You know what?
　你知道嗎？

● Guess what?
　你猜發生什麼事。

相關用法

● Is it true?
　是事實嗎？

● I can't believe it.
　我不相信。

● It can't be.
　不會吧！

Unit 01 介紹朋友認識

I've heard a lot about you.

我聽到很多關於你的事。

Cathy: I think you'll like Jenny. She's my best friend. Oh, here she is.

我想妳會喜歡珍妮的。她是我最好的朋友。喔,她來了。

Cathy: Hi, Jenny, I'd like you to meet Maria.

嗨,珍妮,來見見瑪麗亞。

Jenny: Nice to meet you.

很高興認識妳。

Maria: I've heard a lot about you from Cathy.

我從凱西那裡聽到很多關於妳的事。

Jenny: Nothing bad, I hope.

希望不是壞事。

Maria: Oh no, only good things.

喔,不,只有好事。

1 生活常用
2 辦公室
3 電話
4 購物
5 人際關係
6 客套短語
7 交通
8 問路

延伸用法

● This is Jenny.
這是珍妮。

● This is Jenny, and this is Maria.
這是珍妮，這是瑪麗亞。

● This is Jenny, my best friend.
這是珍妮，我最要好的朋友。

● She is my colleague.
她是我的同事。

● Jenny is my colleague.
珍妮是我的同事。

● We were roommates.
我們以前是室友。

相關用法

● I'd like you to meet Jenny.
我要你認識一下珍妮。

● We went to the same high school.
我們以前是高中同學。

● How do you know Jenny?
你怎麼認識珍妮的？

Unit 02 似曾相識

Haven't we met before?

我們以前沒有見過面嗎？

Jenny : Haven't we met before?
我們以前沒有見過面嗎？

David : I don't think so.
我想應該沒有。

Jenny : You work for IBM, don't you?
你在 IBM 工作，對吧？

David : Yes, that's right.
是啊，沒錯。

Jenny : I think I met you at IBM's party last week.
我想我上星期在 IBM 的宴會上見過你。

David : Oh, really?
喔，真的嗎？

Jenny : Well, anyway, my name is Jenny.
嗯，總之，我的名字是珍妮。

David : Mine's David.
我(的名字)是大衛。

1 生活常用

2 辦公室

3 電話

4 購物

5 人際關係

6 客套短語

7 交通

8 問路

延伸用法

- I think I have seen you around campus.

  我想我在校園見過你。

- Haven't I met you before?

  我以前沒有見過你嗎？

- Have you two met before?

  你們二位以前見過面嗎？

- You look familiar.

  你看起來很面熟。

- Aren't you Mr. White?

  你不是懷特先生嗎？

- Aren't you a friend of Chris?

  你不是克里斯的朋友嗎？

相關用法

- I think we were in the same class.

  我想我們(以前)是同學。

- Don't you work for IBM?

  你不是在IBM工作嗎？

- Did you go to Taiwan High School?

  你是讀台灣高中的嗎？

Unit 03 簡單寒暄

How are you doing?

你好嗎？

David: Hi, Helen.
嗨，海倫。

Helen: Oh, hi, David. How are you doing?
噢，嗨，大衛。你好嗎？

David: Pretty good.
還不錯！

Helen: Are you still working at IBM?
你還在 IBM 工作嗎？

David: Un-huh. You know, Chris Jones works there too now.
是啊！你知道嗎？克里斯‧瓊斯現在也在那裡工作。

Helen: Really? Well, say hi to him for me, OK?
真的？這樣吧，幫我向他問好，好嗎？

David: OK, I will.
好的，我會的。

2
1
1

1 生活常用

2 辦公室

3 電話

4 購物

5 人際關係

6 客套短語

7 交通

8 問路

延伸用法

- How do you do?

  你好嗎？

- How are you?

  你好嗎？

- What's new?

  近來如何？

- How have you been?

  近來好嗎？

相關用法

- Good to see you.

  見到你真好。

- Glad to see you.

  真高興見到你。

- Glad to see you too.

  我也很高興見到你。

Unit 04 附和對方

It's fine with me.

我都可以。

David : Good morning, Helen.
早安，海倫。

Helen : Good morning.
早安。

David : I'm going to the baseball game. Would you like to come?
我要去看棒球賽。妳要來嗎？

Helen : I'd love to.
我願意。

David : Great. Is it OK to invite Jason to the baseball game?
很好。可以邀請杰生去看棒球賽嗎？

Helen : Sure, it's fine with me.
好啊，我都可以。

David : I'll pick you up at your house at two.
我兩點去妳家接妳。

2
1
3

1 生活常用

2 辦公室

3 電話

4 購物

5 人際關係

6 客套短語

7 交通

8 問路

延伸用法

- You bet.

  當然。

- Great.

  很好。

- Of course.

  當然。

- You are right.

  你是對的。

- You are the boss.

  你說了算。

- You are telling me.

  還用得著你說。

相關用法

- It's truth.

  這是事實。

- No doubt about it.

  毫無疑問。

- Whatever you say!

  隨便你！

Unit 05 隨口答腔

I guess so.

我想是吧!

David: Hey, did you hear about us?
嘿,你聽說了我們的事了嗎?

Helen: What happened to you?
你們怎麼啦?

David: Ross and I were broken up.
蘿絲和我分手了。

Helen: Really? Since when?
真的?什麼時候的事?

David: Two weeks ago.
兩個星期前。

Helen: I see. I'm sorry to hear that.
我瞭解。很抱歉聽到這個消息。

David: That's OK. I can ask Mary out now.
沒關係。我現在可以約瑪麗出去了。

Helen: Sure. I guess so.
是啊!我想是吧!

1 生活常用
2 辦公室
3 電話
4 購物
5 人際關係
6 客套短語
7 交通
8 問路

延伸用法

- Really?

  真的？

- Of course!

  當然了！

- Yeah?

  是嗎？

- Good.

  很好！

- You really think so?

  你真的這樣認為？

- It's no big deal.

  沒什麼大不了的。

相關用法

- Just wonderful!

  簡直太棒了！

- It's hard to say.

  很難說。

- Let me see.

  讓我想想。

MP3 096

Unit 06 反問對方

Don't you think so?

你不這麼認為嗎?

David: What happened to you?
你怎麼啦?

Helen: Why?
麼啦?(為什麼這麼問)

David: Why don't you accept the offer?
妳為什麼不接受這個提議?

Helen: It's not my plan.
這不是我的計畫。

David: It's a good deal. Don't you think so?
這是很好的交易。妳不這麼認為嗎?

Helen: Absolutely not.
絕對不是。

David: You idiot.
妳這個笨蛋。

Helen: Hey, there is nothing on your business!
嘿,不關你的事!

2
1
7

1 生活常用

2 辦公室

3 電話

4 購物

5 人際關係

6 客套短語

7 交通

8 問路

延伸用法

- What do you say?

  你覺得呢？

- What's your opinion?

  你的想法呢？

- What's in your mind?

  你在想什麼？

- What do you think?

  你覺得呢？

- Why?

  為什麼？

- Says who?

  誰說的？

相關用法

- You really think so?

  你真的這麼認為？

- What did you just say?

  你說什麼？

- Don't you agree?

  你不同意嗎？

Unit 07 禮貌拒絕

I'd love to, but I have other plans.

我想答應，但是我有其他計畫了。

David: What are you doing now, Susan?
蘇珊，妳現在在做什麼？

Susan: I'm trying to connect Mr. White.
我嘗試要和懷特先生聯絡。

David: Look, do you have any plans this weekend?
聽我說，妳這個週末有空嗎？

Susan: This weekend? Well, I don't know.
這個週末？嗯，我不知道耶！

David: Would you like to go to a movie with me?
妳要和我一起去看電影嗎？

Susan: Well, I'd love to, but I have other plans.
嗯，我想答應，但是我有其他計畫了。

1 生活常用

2 辦公室

3 電話

4 購物

5 人際關係

6 客套短語

7 交通

8 問路

延伸用法

- I'd love to, but I don't think I can.
  我想答應，但是我不認為我可以。
- I'd love to, but I'm afraid I can't.
  我想答應，但是我恐怕無法答應。
- I'll let you know.
  我會再告訴你。
- I have other plans.
  我有其他計畫了。

相關用法

- Maybe some other time.
  改天吧！
- Well, could you make it next week?
  嗯，可以改成下個星期嗎？
- Could we make it another time, say, Sunday?
  我們可以另外約時間嗎？星期天如何？

Unit 08 答應

Sure.

好啊！

David : Do you have any plans tonight?
你今天晚上有事嗎？

Helen : No. Why?
沒有。為什麼（這麼問）？

David : Would you like to have dinner with me?
妳要和我一起用晚餐嗎？

Helen : Sure. What time?
好啊！什麼時間？

David : How about 5 pm?
下午五點如何？

Helen : 5 pm would be fine.
下午五點可以。

David : OK. I'll pick you up at 5pm.
好。我下午五點去接妳。

2 2 1 1 生活常用 2 辦公室 3 電話 4 購物 5 人際關係 6 客套短語 7 交通 8 問路

延伸用法

- Fine.

  好！

- OK.

  好！

- Great.

  好！

- No problem.

  沒問題！

- Sure. Why not?

  好啊！為什麼不要？

- Sure. What time?

  好啊！什麼時間？

相關用法

- That sounds good.

  聽起來不錯！

- That sounds like a nice idea.

  聽起來是個好主意。

- That would be fine.

  應該不錯。

Unit 09 結束話題

I've got to leave.

我要走了。

David : I've heard about your story.
我已經聽說妳的事了。

Helen : Yeah, I've no choice.
是啊,我別無選擇。

David : I can't believe it happens to you.
我不敢相信這件事會發生在妳身上。

Helen : Never mind.
沒關係!

David : OK, I've got to leave.
好了,我要走了。

Helen : Me too.
我也是。

David : See you soon.
再見囉!

Helen : Bye.
拜!

2 2 3
1 生活常用
2 辦公室
3 電話
4 購物
5 人際關係
6 客套短語
7 交通
8 問路

延伸用法

- I've got to get back to work.

  我要回去工作了。

- Well, I really need to be going.

  唔,我真的必須走了!

- It was nice talking to you.

  和你談話真好。

- Well, I'm sure you've got other things to do.

  嗯,我想你一定還有其他的事要做。

- OK, talk to you later.

  好了,下次再和你聊。

相關用法

- Take care.

  保重。

- Have a nice weekend.

  祝你有個愉快的週末。

- Oh, look at the time!

  喔,時間過得真快!

Unit 10 模稜兩可的回答

It could be.

有可能是！

Helen: What do you think of the movie?
你覺得這部電影如何？

David: It was terrific. I'm glad you invited me.
很棒！我很高興妳邀請我。

Helen: Wow, it's going to be raining.
哇，要下雨了。

David: It could be.
有可能是！

Helen: Come on, let's go home.
快一點，我們回家吧！

David: OK. Uh, no!
好啊！喔，不會吧。

Helen: What's the matter? You look upset.
怎麼啦？你看起來很沮喪喔！

David: I've lost my key.
我弄丟我的鑰匙了。

延伸用法

- Maybe.

  可能。

- Not exactly.

  不完全是。

- I guess so.

  我猜也是。

- I'm not so sure.

  我不確定。

- I hope so.

  我希望如此。

- Yes and no.

  也是也不是。

相關用法

- It depends.

  看情形！

- Kind of.

  有一點。

- Sort of.

  有一點。

Unit 11 讚美

Good job.

幹得好！

Jenny : How is everything?

事情都還好吧？

David : Fine. I just finished the annual plans.

不錯。我剛剛完成了年度的計畫。

Jenny : Good job. How about the sales plans?

幹得好！那銷售計畫呢？

David : I just send it to Mr. Jones.

我剛剛寄給瓊斯先生了。

Jenny : Terrific.

很棒！

David : You know, you really can count on me.

妳知道的，妳是可以信賴我的。

Jenny : Yeah, you've been really helpful.

是啊，你真是幫了大忙。

1 生活常用
2 辦公室
3 電話
4 購物
5 人際關係
6 客套短語
7 交通
8 問路

延伸用法

- You are doing well.

  你表現得很好。

- You are great.

  你很棒。

- Well done.

  幹得好！

- Cool.

  酷喔！

- Excellent.

  真不錯！

- Fantastic.

  太好了！

相關用法

- Nice dress.

  不錯的衣服喔！

- Nice tie.

  不錯的領帶喔！

- Good for you.

  對你很好。

Unit 12 聊計畫

What are you doing tonight?

你今晚要做什麼？

David : What are you doing tonight?
妳今晚要做什麼？

Helen : Not much. I have to get ready for my trip.
沒什麼事。我要準備我去旅遊的事。

David : When will you leave?
妳什麼時候離開？

Helen : On Monday morning.
在週一早上。

David : Say, Jenny and I are going out for dinner tonight. Do you want to come?
對了，珍妮和我今晚要出去吃晚餐。妳要來嗎？

Helen : Well, maybe.... Where are you going to have dinner?
嗯，可能吧…！你們要去哪裡吃晚餐？

2 2 9
1 生活常用
2 辦公室
3 電話
4 購物
5 人際關係
6 客套短語
7 交通
8 問路

延伸用法

- Do you have any plans for tonight?
  你今晚有事嗎？
- What are you going to do tonight?
  你今晚有要做什麼嗎？
- What do you want to do tonight?
  你今晚想要做什麼？
- Are you doing anything tonight?
  你今晚有要做什麼事嗎？
- Are you busy tonight?
  你今晚忙嗎？

相關用法

- I've got an idea.
  我有一個主意。
- Why don't we go to a concert?
  我們何不去聽音樂會？
- Let's go to a baseball game.
  我們去看棒球賽。

Unit 13 不敢相信

I can't believe it.

我真是不敢相信！

Jenny : I'm home. What have you done?
我回來了。你做了什麼事？

David : Nothing. I made a sandwich by myself.
沒事啊！我自己做了一個三明治。

Jenny : You did? I can't believe it.
你自己做的？我真是不敢相信！

David : Yeah, try it.
是啊！嚐嚐看吧！

Jenny : It's delicious.
真是好吃。

David : You like it?
妳喜歡(吃)嗎？

Jenny : Of course I do.
我當然喜歡。

1 生活常用
2 辦公室
3 電話
4 購物
5 人際關係
6 客套短語
7 交通
8 問路

延伸用法

- It's impossible.
  不可能！
- Oh, my God.
  喔，我的天啊！
- Really?
  真的嗎？
- It can't be.
  不可能。

Unit 14 期望

> You deserve it.

> 你應得的。

David: Look, honey. I've got a promotion.
聽好，親愛的。我升遷了。

Jenny: Really?
真的嗎？

David: Yes. You know, I work so hard.
是啊。你知道的，我很努力工作的。

Jenny: I'm so happy for you. You deserve it.
我真為你感到高興。你應得的。

David: Let's celebrate it.
我們好好來慶祝一下。

Jenny: Of course.
當然囉！

2
3
3
3

1 生活常用

2 辦公室

3 電話

4 購物

5 人際關係

6 客套短語

7 交通

8 問路

延伸用法

- You make me proud.

  你讓我很驕傲！

- You make me honor.

  你讓我感到榮幸！

- You're a genius.

  你真是天才。

- I trust you.

  我信賴你。

- I believe in you

  我相信你。

Unit 15 失望

I'm so disappointed.

我很失望。

Jenny: You're not going to believe what happened to me.
你不會相信我發生什麼事了。

David: What's wrong?
發生什麼事？

Jenny: Mark and I were separated.
馬克和我分居了。

David: You were?
你們是喔？

Jenny: I'm so disappointed.
我很失望。

David: Hey, it'll work out.
嘿，事情會解決。

Jenny: But he's seeing someone now.
但是他現在有交往的對象了。

2
3
5
1 生活常用
2 辦公室
3 電話
4 購物
5 人際關係
6 客套短語
7 交通
8 問路

延伸用法

- I feel frustrated.

  我覺得很沮喪。

- I feel terrible.

  我覺得糟透了!

- I'm not myself.

  我都不是我自己啦!(我感覺不好)

- I don't think it's a good idea.

  我不覺得是個好主意。

相關用法

- You make me down.

  你讓我很失望。

- How could you do that?

  你怎麼能這麼做?

❷
❸
❼

① 生活常用

② 辦公室

③ 電話

④ 購物

⑤ 人際關係

⑥ 客套短語

⑦ 交通

⑧ 問路

Unit 16 同情

Sorry to hear that.

很遺憾知道這件事。

Jenny: I screwed it up.
我把事情搞砸了。

David: What happened?
發生什麼事？

Jenny: You know what?
你知道嗎？

David: I'm listening.
我在聽。

Jenny: I think I fall in love with someone.
我覺得我愛上某人了。

David: Why? It's good for you.
為什麼？對妳來說很好啊！

Jenny: But he is my brother-in-law.
但是他是我姊夫。

David: Oh, sorry to hear that.
喔，很遺憾知道這件事。

脫口說英語

延伸用法

- I'm sorry to hear that.
  我很遺憾知道這件事。
- I hope it's nothing serious.
  希望情況不會太嚴重。

相關用法

- How awful!
  真是不幸啊!
- How terrible!
  真是悲慘啊!
- What a pity!
  真是可惜啊!
- Gee, that's too bad!
  真是太糟了啊!

Unit 17 打氣

Oh, Come on.

喔，不要這樣。

Jenny : You look upset. Are you OK?
你看起來很沮喪。你還好吧？

David : I was laid off.
我被資遣了。

Jenny : Oh, come on. It's no big deal.
喔，不要這樣。沒什麼大不了。

David : Don't try to comfort me.
不用試圖安慰我。

Jenny : But you can't go on like this.
你不能老這樣下去。

David : How should I tell my wife?
我要如何告訴我太太？

Jenny : Find another job. I believe you can make it.
再找工作。我相信你可以辦得到的。

2
3
9

1 生活常用

2 辦公室

3 電話

4 購物

5 人際關係

6 客套短語

7 交通

8 問路

延伸用法

- It's no problem to you, right?
  對你而言是沒問題的，對吧？
- Keep going.
  繼續努力。
- Make me proud of you.
  要讓我以你為榮。
- Use your gift.
  善用你的天賦。
- Don't underestimate yourself.
  不要低估自己的能力。
- Don't put yourself down.
  不要瞧不起自己。

相關用法

- Where is your ambition?
  你的雄心壯志在哪裡？
- Prove yourself to me.
  向我證明你自己。

Unit 18 認同

I agree with you.

我同意你。

Jenny: So this is what I'm going to do.
所以這就是我要做的事。

David: Maybe you can lower the price.
也許妳可以降低價格。

Jenny: I'll. Because I think it's too ex
pensive.
我會的。因為我覺得太貴了。

David: Yes, I agree with you. When will
you finish the report?
對，我同意妳。妳什麼時候會完成這個
報告？

Jenny: Around two pm, I'd say.
大約下午兩點吧。

David: Send it to me when you finish it.
完成的時候寄給我。

2
4
1

1 生活常用

2 辦公室

3 電話

4 購物

5 人際關係

6 客套短語

7 交通

8 問路

延伸用法

- I agree.

  我同意。

- Bingo.

  答對了！

- That's it.

  沒錯。

- If you say so.

  你說是就是。

- You got it.

  就是如此。

- Correct.

  正確的。

相關用法

- Count me in.

  把我算進去。

- I'm on your side.

  我是站在你這邊的。

Chapter
7 交通

Unit 01 目的地

How can I go to Taipei?

我要如何去台北？

David : Excuse me. May I ask you a question?
抱歉。我可以問妳一個問題嗎？

Jenny : Sure. What's it?
當然可以。什麼事？

David : How can I go to Taipei?
我要如何去台北？

Jenny : You can take number 456 bus.
你可以搭乘 456 號公車。

David : Do I have to change buses?
我應該要換公車嗎？

Jenny : No, you don't.
不，你不需要。

David : OK, thanks. Here is my bus.
好，謝謝。我的公車來了。

Jenny : That's my bus too.
那也是我的公車。

延伸用法

- Where can I catch the bus to Taipei?

  我在哪裡能搭乘到台北的公車？

- Which bus could I get on to Taipei?

  從這裡我應該搭哪一路公車去台北？

- Which way is it to Taipei?

  哪一個方向是到台北的？

- Do you know which line that is on?

  你知道我該坐哪一線呢？

- Does this bus go to Taipei?

  這班公車有到台北嗎？

相關用法

- I'd like to go to Taipei.

  我想要去台北。

- I want to go to Taipei.

  我想去台北。

- I need to get Taipei.

  我需要去台北。

Unit 02 交通工具

Can I get there by bus?

我可以搭乘公車過去嗎？

David: Do you know where the post of fice is?

妳知道郵局在哪裡嗎？

Jenny: It's next to the Taipei Hospital.

就在台北醫院旁邊。

David: Can I get there by bus?

我可以搭乘公車過去嗎？

Jenny: It's not very far from here. You can get there on foot.

離這裡不會很遠。你可以用走的到那裡。

David: Which direction, please?

請問是哪一個方向？

Jenny: That way.

那個方向。

David: Thanks.

多謝！

生活常用 辦公室 電話 購物 人際關係 客套短語 交通 問路

延伸用法

- Is there a subway station nearby?
  這附近有地鐵站嗎？

- Is there a MRT nearby?
  這附近有捷運嗎？

- Can I take the train to get there?
  我能搭火車到那裡嗎？

- Where can I transfer to No.456?
  我在哪裡能換到456號公車？

- Where does the bus to Taipei depart from?
  到台北的公車在哪裡發車？

- Could you tell me how to find bus 456?
  你能告訴我在哪裡搭乘456號公車嗎？

相關用法

- You can get there by transit.
  你可以坐大眾運輸系統到那裡。

- Do you want a lift to Taipei?
  你要搭便車去台北嗎？

Unit 03 公車

How many stops is it from here?

離這裡有多少站？

David : Is the right bus to Taipei?
這是去台北的公車嗎？

Jenny : That's right.
沒錯。

David : How many stops are there from here?
離這裡有多少站？

Jenny : That's the sixth stop.
第六站。

David : I see. By the way, how many stops are there to the Maple Street?
我瞭解。還有，到楓葉街有多少個站？

Jenny : Let me see.... It's the ninth stop.
我想一想…。是第九站。

延伸用法

- Where is the next bus station?

  下一站公車站是哪裏？

- How many stops?

  有多少站？

- How many stops is it to Taipei?

  到台北要幾站？

- Does this bus stop at Taipei station?

  這班公車有在台北車站停靠嗎？

- Where can I get off?

  我要在哪裡下車？

相關用法

- Would you tell me when I get there?

  到的時候可以告訴我一聲嗎？

- I've got to catch the bus.

  我要去趕公車了。

- Here is my bus.

  我的公車來了。

Unit 04 車票

Can I get there by bus?

我可以搭乘公車到那裡嗎？

David : It's pretty far from here.
離這裡很遠！

Jenny : Can I get there by bus?
我可以搭乘公車到那裡嗎？

David : Yes, you can.
是的，你可以。

Jenny : Where can I buy the tickets to Taipei?
哪裡可以買去台北的車票？

David : It's over there.
就在那裡。

Jenny : Thank you so much.
非常感謝！

David : You're welcome.
不客氣。

2
5
1
1 生活常用
2 辦公室
3 電話
4 購物
5 人際關係
6 客套短語
7 交通
8 問路

延伸用法

- Where is the ticket window?
  售票窗口在哪裡?
- One ticket to Taipei, please.
  (買)一張到台北的車票。
- Two one-way tickets to Taipei, please.
  (買)兩張到台北的單程票。
- I'd like to buy a ticket to Taipei, please.
  我要買一張到台北的車票。

相關用法

- Does this train stop at every station?
  這班列車每一站都有停靠嗎?
- Which is the interchange station?
  哪一站是轉乘站?
- What platform does the train leave from?
  火車從什麼月台離站?
- Where is the right exit to Maple Street?
  到楓葉街要走哪一個出口?

Unit 05 步行

Can I get there on foot?

我可以用走的到那裡嗎？

David: Can I get there on foot?
我可以用走的到那裡嗎？

Jenny: Yes, you could walk if you would like.
可以，你想要的話，可以用走的過去。

David: How far is it?
很有多遠？

Jenny: It's just 5 minutes' walk from here.
從這裡只有五分鐘的步行路程。

David: How to get there on foot?
用步行的要如何到那裡？

Jenny: Go straight ahead, and you'll see it on your right.
往前直走，你就會看到在你的右手邊。

David: Thank you so much.
非常感謝妳。

2
5
3

1 生活常用

2 辦公室

3 電話

4 購物

5 人際關係

6 客套短語

7 交通

8 問路

延伸用法

- It only takes 10 minutes to walk there.
  步行到那裡只要十分鐘。

- I can get there on foot in 10 minutes.
  我可以在十分鐘內步行到達那裡。

- It's 10 minutes' walk to go there on foot.
  走路要花十分鐘才能到那裡。

- The town is an hour's walk from here.
  從這裡步行到鎮上有一小時的路程。

相關用法

- It's a long walk from here.
  從這裡走的話，要一段很長的路程。

Unit 06 方位

How to go to the station?

要如何去車站？

David: Excuse me. I don't know where I am.
抱歉。我不知道我現在人在哪裡。

Jenny: Where do you want to go?
你想要去哪裡？

David: How to go to the station?
要如何去車站？

Jenny: Walk down the street and turn right at the intersection ahead.
沿著這條街走，然後在前面的十字路口右轉。

David: By the way, how far is it from here?
順便問一下，從這裡要多遠？

Jenny: It'll take you 5 minutes' walk.
走路會需要五分鐘。

2
5
5

1
生活常用

2
辦公室

3
電話

4
購物

5
人際關係

6
客套短語

7
交通

8
問路

延伸用法

- Could you tell me how to get there?
  你能告訴我怎樣到那裡嗎？
- Should I take a right here?
  要在這裡右轉嗎？
- Should I take a left here?
  要在這裡左轉嗎？
- Go across the street and walk that way.
  穿過街道往那邊走。
- Which direction?
  哪一個方向？

相關用法

- Cross the street.
  到街的對面。
- Turn right at the intersection ahead.
  在前面的十字路口右轉。

Unit 07 距離

Is it far?

會遠嗎?

David: After you get there, make the first right. You'll see it on your left.
妳到了那裡後,在第一個路口右轉。妳會看到在妳的左手邊。

Jenny: You mean next to the station?
你的意思是在車站旁嗎?

David: That's right.
沒錯。

Jenny: On this side?
這一邊嗎?

David: Yes, it is.
是的,沒錯。

Jenny: Is it far?
會遠嗎?

David: No, not at all.
不會,完全不會。

2 5 7

1 生活常用

2 辦公室

3 電話

4 購物

5 人際關係

6 客套短語

7 交通

8 問路

延伸用法

- How far is it from here?

  離這裡有多遠？

- Is it far from the campus?

  離校區遠嗎？

- Is Taipei close to here?

  台北距離這裡近嗎？

- How close are we to Taipei?

  我們離台北有多近？

- How far until we get on the highway?

  我們還有多久會上高速公路？

- How far until we get off the highway?

  我們還要多遠才能下高速公路呢？

相關用法

- It's about 5 miles.

  大約有五公里。

- It's close to the bank.

  距離銀行很近。

- It's quite far away.

  路途很遠。

Unit 08 時間

How long is the ride?

這一趟車程要多久？

David: What time does the train for Taipei leave?

去台北的火車幾點開？

Jenny: It's about 9:30.

大約九點半。

David: How long is the ride?

這一趟車程要多久？

Jenny: Let's see.... It's about 30 minutes.

我想想…。大約卅分鐘。

David: Could you tell me when to get off?

妳能告訴我什麼時候下車嗎？

Jenny: No problem.

沒問題。

David: Thanks a lot.

多謝。

2
5
9
1 生活常用
2 辦公室
3 電話
4 購物
5 人際關係
6 客套短語
7 交通
8 問路

延伸用法

- How long is it to be there?
  到那裡要多久？
- How long does this bus trip take?
  坐公車要多久的時間？
- How long does it take to get there?
  到那裡要多久的時間？
- Is it a long ride?
  車程要很長的時間嗎？
- When will I reach Taipei?
  我什麼時候可以到達台北？
- When can I get to Taipei?
  我什麼時才能到達台北？

相關用法

- It'll take about 20 minutes.
  大約會要需要廿分鐘。
- It usually takes 25 minutes to get there.
  通常需要廿五分鐘才能到達那裡。

Unit 09 發車時間

When will the bus depart?

公車什麼時候開？

David : Which train can I take to Taipei?
我要去台北應該搭哪一班列車？

Jenny : You can take the blue line train.
你可以搭藍線火車。

David : Which platform is it on?
在哪一個月台？

Jenny : It's on the second platform.
在第二月台。

David : I see. When will the train depart?
我瞭解了。火車什麼時候會開？

Jenny : It's about 10:30.
大約 10 點半。

2
6
1

1 生活常用

2 辦公室

3 電話

4 購物

5 人際關係

6 客套短語

7 交通

8 問路

延伸用法

- How long until the train departs?

  火車還要多久才會發車？

- Will we depart on time?

  我們會準時出發嗎？

- How often do the buses run?

  公車每隔多久發一班車？

Unit 10 外籍乘客上計程車

Come on, get in the car.

來吧，上車吧！

David: Are you looking for a taxi?
妳需要搭計程車嗎？

Jenny: Yes, I do.
是的，我需要。

David: Come on, get in the car. Where can I take you?
來吧，上車吧！妳要去哪？

Jenny: Please take me to the Taipei Museum.
請送我到台北博物館。

David: No problem.
沒問題。

Jenny: How long will it take?
請問要多久的時間（才會到達）？

David: About thirty minutes, if there is no traffic jam.
如果不塞車的話，大概要卅分鐘。

1 生活常用
2 辦公室
3 電話
4 購物
5 人際關係
6 客套短語
7 交通
8 問路

Jenny : I see. Thank you.

我瞭解。謝謝。

延伸用法

- Welcome to Taiwan.

  歡迎到台灣。

- Good morning, sir.

  先生，早安。

- Good morning, madam.

  女士，早安。

相關用法

- Where to?

  去哪裡？

- Where do you want to go?

  你想要去哪裡？

Unit 11 表明目的地

City Hall, please.

請到市政府。

David : Where would you like to go?
姊要去哪裡?

Jenny : City Hall, please.
請到市政府。

David : Pardon?
妳說什麼?

Jenny : City Hall.
(去) 市政府。

David : I see.
瞭解。

Jenny : Thank you.
謝謝。

David : It's my pleasure.
我的榮幸。

2
6
5
1 生活常用
2 辦公室
3 電話
4 購物
5 人際關係
6 客套短語
7 交通
8 問路

延伸用法

- Drive me to the airport, please.
  請載我去機場。
- Please take me to the airport.
  請載我去機場。
- To the airport, please.
  請到機場。
- I want to go to the airport.
  我要到機場。
- Take me to the airport, please.
  請載我去機場。
- Please take me to the address on it.
  請載我到上面的這個地址。

相關用法

- Can you get me out there?
  你能不能載我去那邊？
- Could you take me to the nearest post office?
  請載我到最近的郵局好嗎？

MP3 120

2
6
7

1 生活常用
2 辦公室
3 電話
4 購物
5 人際關係
6 客套短語
7 交通
8 問路

Unit 12 司機詢問目的地

Where to?

你要去哪裡?

David : Do you need a ride?
需不需要我載妳啊?

Jenny : Yes, please.
要的,謝謝。

David : Where to?
妳要去哪裡?

Jenny : To the Taipei Museum.
去台北博物館。

David : OK. Please fasten your seat belt.
好的。請繫緊安全帶。

Jenny : No problem.
沒問題。

延伸用法

- Where would you like to go?
  你要去哪裡？
- Where are you going?
  你要去哪裡？
- Where can I take you?
  要我載你去哪裡？
- Which part of Taipei are you going to?
  你要去台北的哪裡？

相關用法

- I can take you there.
  我可以送你過去。
- Sorry, I'm not going that way.
  抱歉，我不是要去那個方向。

- You will have to take another cab.
  你需要搭另一部計程車。

Unit 13 機場接機

I'm in charge of taking you to the hotel.

我負責接送你到飯店。

David: Hello. I'm David. I'm in charge of taking you to the hotel.

哈囉。我是大衛。我負責接送妳到飯店。

Jenny: Nice to meet you!

真高興遇見你。

David: Nice to meet you, too. Let me help you with those bags and luggage.

我也很高興遇見妳。讓我幫妳拿這些袋子和行李。

Jenny: Thanks. That is very kind of you.

謝謝。你真好。

David: You're welcome. Be careful of the cars!

不客氣。小心車子。

2 6 9
1 生活常用
2 辦公室
3 電話
4 購物
5 人際關係
6 客套短語
7 交通
8 問路

延伸用法

- Let me take you to the airport.

  讓我送你去機場。

- I'll drive you to the airport.

  我會載你去機場。

- I'll meet you at the airport.

  我會去機場接機。

相關用法

- I'm a cab driver.

  我是計程車司機。

Unit 14 確認路線

Why are you turning here?

為什麼你要在這裡轉彎?

Jenny: Are you sure we are on the right road?
你肯定我們走的路對嗎?

David: It is faster.
這比較快。

Jenny: Why are you turning here?
為什麼你要在這裡轉彎?

David: I will take a short cut later.
我等一下會抄近路。

Jenny: But I usually don't go this way.
但是我通常都不走這條路。

David: Because this route has less traffic.
因為這個路線車輛較少。

Jenny: Wait a minute, but I'm not going to Taipei.
等一下,但我不是要去台北啊!

2 7 1

1 生活常用
2 辦公室
3 電話
4 購物
5 人際關係
6 客套短語
7 交通
8 問路

延伸用法

- Are you going to Taipei now?

  你現在是往台北方向嗎？

- Where are we now?

  我們現在在哪裡？

- Where is this place?

  這地方是哪裡啊？

Unit 15 到達目的地

Here we are.

我們到了。

Jenny : Is it still much further away?
還很遠嗎？

David : Well...we still have two minutes to go.
嗯...還有兩分鐘就會到。

Jenny : I see. I am in a hurry.
我瞭解。我在趕時間。

（稍後到達目的地）

David : Here we are.
我們到了。

Jenny : Are we? I don't see the TICC.
是嗎？我沒看到國際會議中心。

David : Look, it's just in front of you.
看，就在妳面前。

Jenny : Oh, I see.
喔，我瞭解。

2
7
3

1 生活常用

2 辦公室

3 電話

4 購物

5 人際關係

6 客套短語

7 交通

8 問路

延伸用法

- It'll need another 20 minutes.
  還要再廿分鐘。
- We're getting close.
  我們快到了。
- We'll be there in plenty of time.
  我們到那裡的時間綽綽有餘。

相關用法

- Is this your destination?
  你的目的地是這裡嗎？

Unit 16 確認車資

How much is the fare?

車資是多少？

Jenny: How long will it take to get there?
　　　到那裡要多久的時間？

David: Let's see.... It's about fifteen minutes.
　　　我看看…。大概十五分鐘。

Jenny: I see. Thank you.
　　　我了解了。謝謝你。

（稍後到達目的地）

David: Here you are.
　　　到了。

Jenny: IIow much is the fare?
　　　車資是多少？

David: It's two hundred and fifty dollars.
　　　總共二百五十元。

延伸用法

- How much is it?

  多少錢？

- How much did you say?

  你説多少錢？

- How much are you saying?

  你是説多少錢？

- How much should I pay?

  我應該付多少錢？

相關用法

- It's two hundred.

  兩百(元)。

- It's two hundred dollars.

  兩百元。

- Two hundred, please.

  兩百(元)，謝謝。

Unit 17 放行李

Let me put your luggage in.

讓我幫你把行李放進去。

David: Hello! Where to?
哈囉！去哪裡？

Jenny: Taipei Hotel, please.
請到台北飯店。

David: Let me open the trunk.
讓我打開行李廂。

Jenny: Thanks a lot.
多謝啦！

David: No problem. Let me put your luggage in.
沒問題的。讓我幫妳把行李放進去。

Jenny: You're so nice.
你真好心。

David: It's my pleasure.
我的榮幸。

延伸用法

- Let me help you.
  我來幫你!
- Allow me.
  我來(幫你)吧!
- Let me help you with that suitcase.
  我來幫你拿那個行李吧!
- Let me put your baggage in the trunk.
  我來把你的行李放在行李廂內。
- Let's place your suitcases in the rear seat.
  我們把你的行李放在後座吧!

相關用法

- Sorry, my cab is not so big enough.
  抱歉,我的計程車不夠大。
- Those big suitcases won't fit in the trunk.
  那些行李不適合放在行李廂。
- I'm not sure if they will all fit.
  我不確定它們是否全塞得進去。

Chapter

8 問路

Unit 01 想去哪裡？

Where do you want to go?

你想要去哪裡？

Jenny : I don't know where I am!
我不知道我現在在哪裡。

David : OK, just relax. I'll help you.
好的，放輕鬆。我會幫妳的。

Jenny : Thank you so much.
太感謝你了。

David : Where do you want to go?
妳想要去哪裡？

Jenny : I'm looking for the Hilton Hotel.
我在找希爾頓飯店。

David : Are you? You are in front of the Hilton Hotel, ma'am.
是喔？女士，妳就在希爾頓飯店前面。

1 生活常用
2 辦公室
3 電話
4 購物
5 人際關係
6 客套短語
7 交通
8 問路

延伸用法

- Where are you going?
  你要去哪裡？
- Where do you want to know?
  你想知道哪裡？
- Where are you trying to be?
  你試著要去哪裡？
- Where would you like to be?
  你想去哪裡？

相關用法

- I'll help you.
  我會幫你。
- It's not very far from here.
  離這裡不會很遠。

Unit 02 迷路了

I'm lost.

我迷路了。

Jenny : Do you need help?
你需要幫助嗎?

David : Yes, please. I'm lost.
是的,麻煩你了。我迷路了。

Jenny : It's OK. Where do you want to go?
沒關係。你想要去哪裡?

David : I need to go to the museum.
我需要去博物館。

Jenny : Museum? Which museum?
博物館?哪一個博物館?

David : Oh, it's the History Museum.
喔,是歷史博物館。

Jenny : OK. Turn right, and you'll see it.
好的。右轉,然後你就會看見。

1 生活常用
2 辦公室
3 電話
4 購物
5 人際關係
6 客套短語
7 交通
8 問路

延伸用法

- I don't know where I am!
  我不知道我現在在哪裡。
- Where am I?
  我在哪裡？
- Where am I on this map?
  我在這張地圖上的哪裡？
- Do you know where I am?
  你知道我人在哪裡嗎？

Unit 03 問路

Can I get some directions?

我能問一下路嗎？

Jenny : Excuse me, can you do me favor?
抱歉，你能幫我一個忙嗎？

David : Sure. What can I do for you?
當然可以。我可以幫妳什麼忙？

Jenny : Can I get some directions?
我能問一下路嗎？

David : Where are you trying to go?
妳想要去哪裡？

Jenny : Do you know where the museum is?
你知道博物館在哪裡嗎？

David : The museum? Oh, yes, it's on Fox Street.
博物館？喔，知道，在福斯街。

Jenny : Where is the Fax Street?
福斯街在哪裡？

2
8
5

1 生活常用

2 辦公室

3 電話

4 購物

5 人際關係

6 客套短語

7 交通

8 問路

延伸用法

- Can you direct me to the museum?
  你能告訴我去博物館怎麼走嗎？
- Would you tell me how to go to the museum?
  你能告訴我如何去博物館嗎？
- Would you show me how to go to the museum?
  你能告訴我如何去博物館嗎？
- Where can I take a taxi?
  我可以在哪裡搭乘計程車？

相關用法

- I am lost.
  我迷路了。
- Where am I on this map?
  我在地圖上的哪裡？
- What street am I on?
  我在哪一條街上？

Unit 04 找特定地點

I'm looking for Citibank.

我在找花旗銀行。

Jenny : Excuse me.
請問一下。

David : Yes?
什麼事？

Jenny : I'm looking for Citibank.
我在找花旗銀行。

David : Citibank? It's on Roosevelt Road.
花旗銀行？就在就在羅斯福路上。

Jenny : Is that the road that's parallel to Maple?
是和楓葉(街)平行的那一條路嗎？

David : No, it's parallel to Global Street.
不是，是和全球街平行。

Jenny : Oh, I see. Thank you.
喔，我瞭解。謝謝你。

2
8
7
1 生活常用
2 辦公室
3 電話
4 購物
5 人際關係
6 客套語
7 交通
8 問路

延伸用法

- Where is the shoe store?
  鞋店在哪裡？
- How do I get to the station?
  我要怎麼去車站？
- Can you show me the library?
  你能告訴我圖書館在哪裡嗎？
- Could you direct me to the City Hall?
  你能指示我市政府怎麼去嗎？

相關用法

- I don't know where the museum is.
  我不知道博物館在哪裡。
- Do you know where the theater is?
  你知道戲劇院在哪裡嗎？

Unit 05 找特定地點做某事

Where can I get something to eat?

我可以到哪裡找些東西吃？

David: Where can I get something to eat?

我可以到哪裡找些東西吃？

Jenny: There's a restaurant at the end of the corridor.

在走廊的盡頭有一家餐廳。

David: And I'll have to buy some souvenirs.

還有我會需要買一些紀念品。

Jenny: There're lots of souvenir shops nearby.

附近有很多紀念品販賣店。

David: Really? Where exactly?

真的嗎？確切的位置在哪裡？

Jenny: In fact, there's one very close to your hotel.

事實上，有一間離你的飯店非常近。

延伸用法

- Where can I change some money?
  我可以在哪裡兌換錢幣？
- Where should I get my hair cut?
  我應該到哪裡剪我的頭髮？
- Is there a place near here where I can buy some souvenirs?
  這附近哪裡可以買到一些紀念品？

相關用法

- There's a bank down the corridor.
  有一間銀行在走廊的最後。
- There's a bank opposite the coffee shop.
  在咖啡館對面有一間銀行。
- There's a bank next to the coffee shop.
  在咖啡館旁邊有一間銀行。
- There's a bank near the coffee shop.
  在咖啡館附近有一間銀行。

Unit 06 不確定地點

I'm not sure where it is.

我不確定在哪裡。

Jenny：Excuse me, but I'm lost.
抱歉，我迷路了。

David：Where are you looking for?
妳要找哪裡？

Jenny：I'm going to the theater.
我要去劇院。

David：The theater? Sorry, I'm not sure
where it is.
劇院？我不確定它在哪裡。

Jenny：Thank you anyway.
總之還是謝謝你。

David：You're welcome.
不客氣。

1 生活常用

2 辦公室

3 電話

4 購物

5 人際關係

6 客套短語

7 交通

8 問路

延伸用法

● Sorry, I don't know.
抱歉，我不知道。

● I have no idea.
我不知道。

● I'm a tourist too.
我也是遊客。

相關用法

● Let me ask somebody for you.
我幫你問別人。

Unit 07 往前直走

Go straight ahead.

往前直走。

Jenny : Excuse me, I'm lost. Can you help me, please?

請問一下，我迷路了。能請你幫我嗎？

David : Sure.

當然好。

Jenny : Where is the MRT entrance?

捷運站入口在哪裡？

David : Go straight ahead to the second intersection, cross the street, and you'll see it.

往前直走一直到第二個路口，穿過街道，然後你就會看見。

Jenny : Go straight ahead? Thank you so much.

往前直走嗎？非常感謝。

2
9
3

1 生活常用

2 辦公室

3 電話

4 購物

5 人際關係

6 客套短語

7 交通

8 問路

延伸用法

- Go straight ahead.
  往前直走。
- Go straight ahead to Maple Street.
  往前直走到楓葉街。
- Go straight ahead at the traffic lights and then turn right.
  往前直走到紅綠燈，然後右轉。
- Go straight ahead. There is a coffee shop next to the newsagent.
  往前直走。在報攤旁邊有一間咖啡館。

Unit 08 往前直走然後左轉

Go straight ahead and turn left.

往前直走然後左轉。

David : Excuse me. I'm looking for the First Theater.

請問一下。我在找第一劇院。

Jenny : Yes?

然後？

David : Where am I supposed to go?

我應該往哪裡走？

Jenny : Go straight ahead and turn left. You'll see it on the left.

往前直走然後左轉。你就會看到在邊。

David : Where to turn left?

在哪裡左轉？

Jenny : Turn left when you get to the park.

到公園的時候左轉。

David : I see. Thank you.

我瞭解了。謝謝妳。

脫口說英語

延伸用法

- Go straight ahead, and then turn right.

  往前直走然後右轉。

- Go straight until you see a shoe shop.

  往前直走直到你看見鞋店。

- Cross the street to the newsagent.

  穿越街道到報攤。

相關用法

- Turn right and walk three blocks.

  右轉然後走過三個街區。

- Turn first right at the end of the street.

  在街道盡頭的第一處右轉。

- Turn right at the next street.

  在下一條街道右轉。

Unit 09 走到特定地點

Go to that corner.

到那個角落。

Jenny: Can you show me the 101 Building?

你能告訴我 101 大樓在哪裡嗎？

David: You can't see it from here. Do you see that very old building on the corner?

妳在這裡看不到。妳有看見角落那個很舊的建築物嗎？

Jenny: Is it a brick building?

是磚砌的建築物嗎？

David: Yes, that's the one. Go to that corner. Turn right and walk about three blocks.

對，就是那一個。到那個角落。右轉然後走三個街區。

Jenny: Then?

然後呢？

2 9 7

1 生活常用
2 辦公室
3 電話
4 購物
5 人際關係
6 客套短語
7 交通
8 問路

David : Look left. You'll see 101 Building from there.

往左看。妳就會在那裡看見 101 大樓。

延伸用法

● Go to the red brick building.
走到紅色磚砌的建築物。

● Go to the building with the round roof before the park.
走到公園之前的圓頂大樓。

相關用法

● It's that way.
那條路。

● Look right.
往右看。

● Look left.
往左看。

Unit 10 右轉

Turn right.

右轉。

Jenny: Where can I find a public tele phone around here?

我可以在這附近的哪裡找到公共電話？

David: Turn right and go straight ahead.

右轉然後直走。

Jenny: Turn right and go straight ahead?

右轉然後直走嗎？

David: Yes, keep going and you'll see it.

是的，繼續走你就會看見。

Jenny: For how long?

要多久？

David: About 10 minutes. There is a telephone at the coffee shop.

大約十分鐘。在咖啡館有一個電話。

1 生活常用
2 辦公室
3 電話
4 購物
5 人際關係
6 客套短語
7 交通
8 問路

延伸用法

- Turn left.

  左轉。

- Just turn right.

  只要右轉。

- Just turn left.

  只要左轉。

- Turn right at the next street.

  在下一條街右轉。

- Turn left on Maple Street.

  在楓葉街右轉。

- Take a right onto Sixth Street.

  右轉進入第六街。

相關用法

- Turn right and you'll see it.

  右轉你就會看見。

- At the end of the ramp take a left.

  在斜坡的盡頭左轉。

Unit 11 在右邊

It's on your right side.

就在你的右手邊。

Jenny：I don't know where I am.
　　　　 我不知道我在哪裡。

David：Where are you trying to go?
　　　　 你想要去哪裡？

Jenny：Do you know where the museum is?
　　　　 你知道博物館在哪裡嗎？

David：The museum? Oh, yes, it's on Fox Street.
　　　　 博物館？喔，對，在福斯街。

Jenny：How to get there?
　　　　 要怎麼到那裡？

David：Keep walking down the street for 10 minutes. It's on your right side.
　　　　 這條街繼續走十分鐘。就在你的右手邊。

Jenny：Thank you so much.
　　　　 非常感謝！

3 0 1

① 生活常用
② 辦公室
③ 電話
④ 購物
⑤ 人際關係
⑥ 客套短語
⑦ 交通
⑧ 問路

延伸用法

● It's on your left side.

就在你的左手邊。

● It's on your right.

就在你的右邊。

● It's on your left.

就在你的左邊。

● It's on the right.

就在右邊。

● It's on the left.

就在左邊。

相關用法

● It's on the right side of the building.

在建築物的右邊。

● It's on the left side of the apartment.

在公寓的左邊。

Unit 12 繼續往前走

Keep walking down the street.

這條街繼續走。

Jenny : I'm going to the hospital.
我要去醫院。

David : You're going the wrong way.
妳走錯路了。

Jenny : Can you show me on the map?
你能幫我在地圖上指出來嗎？

David : Sure. You're over here. Keep wal king down the street for about 5 minutes.
當然好。妳在這裡。在這條街繼續走大約五分鐘。

Jenny : And then?
然後呢？

David : You'll see it on the left side.
妳就會看到在左邊。

Jenny : Thanks. It's very nice of you.
多謝！你真好。

3 0 3

1 生活常用

2 辦公室

3 電話

4 購物

5 人際關係

6 客套短語

7 交通

8 問路

延伸用法

- Keep walking down.

  繼續往下走。

- Keep walking down on the street.

  繼續在這條街往下走。

- Go one more block to the inter-section of Farm Road and Maple Street.

  再過一個街區到農場路和楓葉街的路口。

Unit 13 不會找不到

You can't miss it.

你不會找不到的。

Jenny : Excuse me. Can you help me?
抱歉。你可以幫我忙嗎？

David : Sure. What's it?
當然可以。什麼事？

Jenny : Where is the police station?
警察局在哪裡？

David : Let me see.... Go straight ahead for two blocks, and you will see it on the left side.
我想想…。直走兩個街區，然後妳就會看到在左邊。

Jenny : On the left side?
在左邊？

David : Yes, you can't miss it.
對，妳不會找不到的。

1 生活常用
2 辦公室
3 電話
4 購物
5 人際關係
6 客套短語
7 交通
8 問路

延伸用法

- You'll find it.
  你就會看見。
- You won't miss it.
  你不會錯過的。
- You'll see a tall, white building.
  你會看見一個高的白色建築物。

相關用法

- That's it.
  就是它。
- That's right.
  沒錯。
- Yes, it is.
  是的,就是它。
- Yes, that's the one.
  是的,就是那一個。

Unit 14 相對位置

It's next to the hospital.

就在醫院旁邊。

Jenny: Can you help me?
你能幫我嗎？

David: Yes, ma'am.
是的，女士。

Jenny: Which one is the SOGO Building?
哪一棟是 SOGO 大樓？

David: It's next to the hospital.
就在醫院旁邊。

Jenny: Where is the hospital?
醫院在哪裡？

David: It's over there. See?
就在那裡。看見了嗎？

Jenny: Oh, right. I see it.
喔，對。我看見了。

1 生活常用
2 辦公室
3 電話
4 購物
5 人際關係
6 客套短語
7 交通
8 問路

延伸用法

● It's in front of the gallery.

在美術館前面。

● It's across the hospital.

在醫院對街處。

● It's between the bank and the restaurant.

在銀行和餐廳中間。

● It's close to the beach.

離海灘很近。

MP3 140

3
0
9

1 生活常用
2 辦公室
3 電話
4 購物
5 人際關係
6 客套短語
7 交通
8 問路

Unit 15 容易找到

That sounds easy.

聽起來很簡單。

David : Excuse me. Do you know where the 101 Building is?
請問一下。你知道 101 大樓在哪裡嗎？

Jenny : Yes, it's that way. Straight ahead.
是的，在那個方向。往前直走。

David : Just straight ahead?
只要往前直走？

Jenny : Yes, go straight ahead towards Maple Avenue and turn right.
是的，往楓葉大道的方向往前直走然後右轉。

David : And then?
然後呢？

Jenny : It's next to the MRT entrance.
就在捷運入口旁邊。

David : Thanks. That sounds easy.
謝謝。聽起來很簡單。

延伸用法

- It seems easy to find it.

  好像很簡單就會找到。

- Very clear. Thanks.

  很清楚。多謝！

- Great. Thanks a lot.

  很好。多謝啦！

相關用法

- It's about 200 meters, on your right.

  大約20公尺，在你的右邊。

- It's on your right side.

  在你的右邊。

- It's not very far away from here.

  離這裡不會很遠。

Unit 16 走哪一條路？

Which way is the post office?

哪一條路可以到郵局？

David: Excuse me. Which way is the post office?

請問一下。哪一條路可以到郵局？

Jenny: The post office? Sorry, I'm not really sure.

郵局。抱歉，我不太確定。

David: Thank you anyway.

總之還是謝謝你。

Jenny: Maybe you can ask the police officer.

也許你可以問警察。

David: Sure, I'll. Thanks again.

會的，我會。再次感謝。

Jenny: You are welcome.

不客氣。

3
1
1

1 生活常用

2 辦公室

3 電話

4 購物

5 人際關係

6 客套短語

7 交通

8 問路

延伸用法

- Could you show me the way to the police station?

  你可以告訴我到警察局的路嗎？

- Is there a public toilet around here?

  這裡有沒有公共廁所？

- Where's the nearest police station?

  最近的警察局在哪裡？

Unit 17 街道名字

Which one is the Global Street?

哪一條是全球街？

David：May I help you, ma'am?

女士，需要我幫忙嗎？

Jenny：Yes, please. I don't know where I am.

是的，謝謝。我不知道我在哪裡。

David：You are on the Maple Street.

妳在楓葉街。

Jenny：And which one is the Global Street?

那麼哪一條是全球街？

David：It's 2 blocks away from here.

離這裡有兩個街區遠。

Jenny：Which direction?

在哪一個方向？

David：That way.

那裡。

3
1
3

1 生活常用

2 辦公室

3 電話

4 購物

5 人際關係

6 客套短語

7 交通

8 問路

Jenny：Thank you. You've been very helpful.

謝謝你。你幫了我一個大忙。

延伸用法

- What's the name of this street?

  這條街叫什麼名字？

- Where is the Maple Street?

  楓葉街在哪裡？

- I couldn't find the Maple Street.

  我找不到楓葉街。

- I'm looking for the Maple Street.

  我在找楓葉街。

生活單字萬用手冊

你一定不知道do這個單字多好用！

好用例句1 逛街 do the shopping

好用例句2 做家事 do the housework

好用例句3 熨燙衣服 do the ironing

好用例句4 清洗 do the washing

好用例句5 清潔 do the cleaning

好用例句6 洗碗 do the dishes

只會簡單的單字，也可以開口說英語！

單字急救包

您可以塞在袋裡，放在車上，或是擱在角落。

不管是等公車的通勤族，還是上廁所前培養情緒，隨手抽出本書，就可以利用瑣碎的時間充實一下。

小小一本，大大好用！

台北 PAPAGO！跟老外介紹台北

結合熱門的台北旅遊地點，搭配實用的英文旅遊會話，讓您在熟悉的情境中記憶並活用英文旅遊短句與字彙，輕鬆用英文介紹台北的吃喝玩樂。

一天 10 分鐘的時間，

學英文變得更輕鬆。

永續圖書
線上購物網

www.foreverbooks.com.tw

◆ 加入會員即享活動及會員折扣。

◆ 每月均有優惠活動，期期不同。

◆ 新加入會員三天內訂購書籍不限本數金額，
　即贈送精選書籍一本。（依網站標示為主）

專業圖書發行、書局經銷、圖書出版

永續圖書總代理：

五觀藝術出版社、培育文化、棋茵出版社、犬拓文化、讀
品文化、雅典文化、知音人文化、手藝家出版社、璞申文
化、智學堂文化、語言鳥文化

活動期內，永續圖書將保留變更或終止該活動之權利及最終決定權。

脫口說英語：基礎篇

親愛的顧客您好，感謝您購買這本書。即日起，填寫讀者回函卡寄回至
本公司，我們每月將抽出一百名回函讀者，寄出精美禮物並享有生日當
月購書優惠！想知道更多更即時的消息，歡迎加入"永續圖書粉絲團"
您也可以選擇傳真、掃描或用本公司準備的免郵回函寄回，謝謝。

傳真電話：（02）8647-3660　　　　電子信箱：yungjiuh@ms45.hinet.net

姓名：	性別：	□男　□女
出生日期：　年　　月　　日	電話：	
學歷：	職業：	
E-mail：		
地址：□□□		
從何處購買此書：	購買金額：	元
購買本書動機：□封面 □書名 □排版 □內容 □作者 □偶然衝動		
你對本書的意見： 內容：□滿意□尚可□待改進　　編輯：□滿意□尚可□待改進 封面：□滿意□尚可□待改進　　定價：□滿意□尚可□待改進		
其他建議：		

總經銷：永續圖書有限公司

永續圖書線上購物網
www.foreverbooks.com.tw

您可以使用以下方式將回函寄回。

您的回覆，是我們進步的最大動力，謝謝。

① 使用本公司準備的免郵回函寄回。

② 傳真電話：（02）8647-3660

③ 掃描圖檔寄到電子信箱：

　　yungjiuh@ms45.hinet.net

沿此線對折後寄回，謝謝。

2 2 1 0 3

 雅典文化事業有限公司　收

新北市汐止區大同路三段194號9樓之1

雅致風靡　典藏文化